INTRIGUE ON THE UPPER LEVEL

By
THOMAS TEMPLE HOYNE

ARMCHAIR FICTION
PO Box 4369, Medford, Oregon 97504

The original text of this novel was first published by the Reilly and Lee Company.

For more information about Armchair Books and products, visit our website at…

www.armchairfiction.com

Or email us at…

armchairfiction@yahoo.com

A DESPERATE STRUGGLE FOR POWER IN 2050 A. D.

James Manse lived on the shore of Lake Michigan with thousands of other homeless souls in the shadows of the magnificent structures of the Upper Level. Like so many others of his ilk, he longed for the opportunity to advance his position in life and somehow gain entrance to those spectacular, lofty structures that were so near, yet so unreachable. Then one day a simple act of heroism thrust Jimmy Manse from the lowest reaches of humanity to the highest pinnacle of human extravagance. He soon found himself in the company of the Master, the most powerful man on Earth. But in this ruthless dictator he saw a man enveloped by fear, desperately striving to stave off a massive rebellion that seemed impossible to stop.

"Intrigue on the Upper Level" is a forgotten gem of futuristic science fiction, laced with thought provoking themes, intertwined with nail-biting action and intrigue—and not seen in print since 1934.

CAST OF CHARACTERS

JAMES MANSE

This idealist lived on a beach with countless others, dreaming of a life on the Upper Level—a dream that would soon come true.

VIVIAN RANSLER

As the daughter of the Master she was could have anything she wanted—a fringe benefit she indulged herself in often.

GEORGE RANSLER

He was the Master of the Upper Level, a position he had attained through cunning brutality—and making his enemies disappear.

DR. FINLEY P. EDGERTON

He came to the Ransler palace along with Jimmy Manse—but only he understood the real significance of what was happening.

MIRIAM ESTLEY

As a modern day Joan of Arc, she played a dangerous part in the revolutionary uprising against the Upper Level.

FRANKLYN EBETS

As one of the Master's top banking executives, he held a powerful, coveted position. Yet why did he seem so…nervous?

BROMWELL

Just like an old, faithful dog, his sole purpose was to do the Master's bidding.

CHAPTER ONE

THE first rays of the rising sun on July 4, 2050, darted across the glassy level of Lake Michigan and roused twenty-four year old Jimmy Manse, sleeping on the narrow Oak street beach. He sat up and looked around with dull interest.

Well he knew what the dawn would reveal. Morning after morning he had gazed at the same scene. Thousands of the unemployed lying all about him in the yellow sand with their feet toward the lake—unmated men of the educated proletariat huddled in the ugly attitudes of sleep.

Behind him, he knew how the first faint glow of day was already sharpening the hard, jagged skyline of the city's mighty shafts and cubes of tinted glassite, stone and steel, towering in the early light like an impregnable fortress.

He twisted his head and studied again that formidable defense of wealth and power. Those double-decked boulevards, connecting with the broad drive along the lake shore, divided life in the metropolis like a horizontal plane of steel. Above, riches, luxury, boundless extravagance; crime and vice better concealed; murder less flagrant; indecency less public. Below, idleness and ill-paid toil, sullen anger, bitter envy, raging futility.

There on the Upper Level lay opportunity, fortune, mastery. He felt his teeth grit as unconsciously he clenched his jaws with determination. He, Jimmy Manse, resident of the Lower Level, fed at free civic restaurants, lodged in free municipal lodging-houses or on the open beach like an animal—he, Jimmy Manse, would yet storm those heights and wrest for himself some of that power so jealously guarded.

His eyes swept back toward the sunrise. It threatened a gloomy day. Already the upper edge of the blood-orange disk was slipping behind waiting clouds, before the lower edge had risen above the water.

Jimmy reached out and lightly shook the sleeper next to him, a man of sixty, who lay on his back, mouth open, purring in peaceful slumber.

"The sun is looking us over," said Jimmy in a low mocking voice. "Are you without shame? Up and rejoice! This is the glorious Fourth of July."

Doctor Finley P. Edgerton, recipient of high educational honors, former professor in the department of philosophy at the University of Chicago, responded sluggishly. Nevertheless he sat up, wiping wind-blown grains of sand from his face with the palm of his hand, and looked out across the glassy lake.

"Don't try to be sarcastic, my boy," he murmured. "It suggests the futile scholarship of these modern beachcombers who lie all around us. Hardly one of them lacks at least a master's degree from some noble university and a refined disgust for the Fourth of July."

Jimmy drew himself out of the heavy paper sleeping bag that encased his body up to the armpits and stripped to the bathing suit that served also as underwear.

"Watch my clothes," he genially commanded and began to thread his way toward the water.

Even on this beach where the sleepers were men of high education it was advisable to cooperate in pairs for mutual protection against petty theft.

Dr. Edgerton crawled out of his own sleeping bag, and fished into it to bring up soap, towel, brush, comb, shaving utensils. By the time he was ready for his plunge, Jimmy was back.

When the doctor returned from his bath, the younger man, already dressed and shaved, was packing away his few toilet articles.

The sun had altogether disappeared behind clouds that postponed broad daylight. The quiet air lacked its usual morning freshness, but tingled with invisible rays of impending storm.

"Rain sure," proclaimed Jimmy. "Hurry up, doctor!"

It was nearly as dark as before the sun had risen. A low growl of thunder caused Dr. Edgerton to look up at the black sky.

"Yes," he agreed; "Nature carries through after a warning. Our forefathers did that in 1776."

"Some of us do it yet."

"Bosh!" replied the older man. "Not down here in this underworld of ours, they don't. Up on the Upper Level, yes. But down here we're a mass of jellyfish humanity enervated by our own feeble threats."

Jimmy smiled, as the doctor continued vehemently. "Men have always been free to do what they pleased, if they were capable of doing it. We're in the same fix now, and most of us still unable to do anything with our freedom. The really strong are all up on the Upper Level—or eventually get there."

"I'm going to get there, too!" snapped Jimmy.

"An old colloquialism!" answered the other. "Talk and a university education won't do it."

"What about ability?" asked the young man sharply.

"The right kind will; but I doubt if you have it. I can't make you understand that civilization has moved forward to the effete state of parasitism. You're a wholesome boy with an athletic, handsome body, and a mind unvitiated by mass education. You don't want to be a parasite. You think you can be a commander without earning your commission as a sycophant. That can't be done, unless you're a daring criminal; and there inherent honesty bars your progress."

"No hope for me, you think?" Jimmy's eyes were bright with humor.

"My boy, I'm cursed with honesty, too. It was that, and love of my own independence of mind, that forced my resignation from the university. Compared with getting near the top in the boiling life of the Upper Level, attaining eminence as a purveyor of predigested educational pap is child's play. I'm too old to begin life over again, but I can tell you facts."

Dr. Edgerton finished strapping up the sleeping bag containing his belongings, and rose to his feet as a louder peal of thunder rumbled distantly. He looked down at Jimmy seated in the sand, with the quiet city behind him.

"You're a throwback to a barbarous and decent past, James—to about the grandly stupid Victorian era, I should say. You're obsessed with integrity, loyalty, chivalry and other outworn beliefs. You're a monogamist, a one-woman man practicing rigid chastity, and—worst of all—I suspect you're in love."

The young fellow's face flushed, and he ejaculated with some asperity. "Your advice, professor?"

"I would not advise you," rejoined the doctor. "But I will tell you positively that in any age attainment of success—without genius—begins with recognition and observance of the law that directs the social evolution of the times. Today that law is parasitism. To succeed, gain some powerful tycoon as your patron. Make yourself pleasing to him, if only by flattering his attention with feigned enthusiasm for his worst vice or silliest hobby. Better still," he added, raising his eyes toward the Upper Level, "make some woman up there—who has power—desire you. There—"

He stopped speaking. Jimmy whirled round to follow the doctor's gaze.

A woman was coming down the narrow stairway from the upper drive. The heavy door at the top, which shut off ingress to the Upper Level unless the proper tax-card were presented, had been closed and presumably locked behind her by the guard on duty.

In spite of the murky dimness, it was possible to distinguish the lines of her evening gown, to discern jewels on her bare neck, arms and fingers. Young, beautiful, she was coming down the stairway with proud, erect carriage, her left hand lightly resting on the railing, reminiscent of an ancient portrait of the Princess Louise.

To descend from the Upper Level at such an hour was more than dangerous for a woman unaccompanied. It was reckless!

The two observers could see a man, lurking under the stairway, tensely watching the hand that slid slowly down the rail. On the wrist gleamed a diamond bracelet. Behind him other sinister figures grouped in the shadow, waiting.

Manse and the doctor were not the only spectators. Here and there on the beach an awakened sleeper, strangely aware of what was taking place, rolled over on his breast and lifted his head, the better to watch what he knew was going to happen.

The man beneath the stairway edged out and forward, as the hand on the rail moved down within his reach. Suddenly he seized it, pulled the arm toward him over the railing, and tried to tear the bracelet from the wrist.

No scream of fear came from the girl's lips, only a short cry of surprise. Dragged close against the rail, she leaned over and drove her small, right fist into the face of her assailant again and again.

Three other figures slid out from under the stairs to join the attack.

Not even a murmur of protest arose from the spectators lying in the sand. Here and there a head lifted higher, but no man so much as rose to his feet until Manse sprang up, shook off Dr. Edgerton's restraining hand, and rushed into the petty melee. The doctor picked up his light walking stick, and followed with less ardor.

Jimmy swung heavily on the powerful fellow trying to loosen the bracelet, breaking his grip and knocking him down. He dashed up the stairs toward the girl, who was now fighting another assailant with the fury of a cat. Seizing the collar of the man close upon her, Jimmy wrenched him backward down the steps. The catapulting body blocked for a moment the advance of two others.

Dr. Edgerton was close behind Jimmy.

"Up the stairs with her!" he cried, and turned, cane in hand, to face the four thieves coming on again. Others of their kind were slinking out from the dark roadway under the upper drive. On the beach a few men were beginning to rise to their feet, ready to join the pack closing in on so rich a quarry.

The doctor waited for no oncoming rush. The stairway was built narrow and steep to make mob attack on the Upper Level difficult. He did not use his stick as a club, but as a fencer would use a foil, stabbing with lightning speed, at throat, mouth and eye.

His defense would at best have been short-lived, if the guard had not opened the door at the top and run down the steps, his gas tank on his back and mask over his face. Across the doctor's shoulder he thrust the nozzle of the hose from the tank and pressed the trigger. A hissing stream of riot-gas poured into the faces of the closest adversaries. They dropped like flies swept by flame. The growing mob behind them broke, and scattered in panic.

Before the attack could be renewed, the girl and her rescuers were through the door at the top of the stairs, and the guard had slammed and locked it.

"I warned you not to go down there alone, madam," he said respectfully, like one establishing a fact before witnesses.

She paid no attention to him. Her eyes were blazing with excitement—almost ecstasy. She looked down at her left wrist, cut by the bracelet and bleeding. Lifting it quickly to her mouth, she thrust out a red, pointed tongue, and licked up the blood with animal relish.

The guard turned to the two men.

"Your tax-cards?" he asked civilly.

The young woman forestalled their reply.

"I'll sign a voucher for their responsibility."

To Manse she announced with hauteur that did not conceal her satisfaction with his appearance:

"My name is Vivian Ransler. I'm the daughter of George Ransler."

Both men well knew who George Ransler was. His name was a shibboleth, representing invisible power that drove the machinery governing the nation to suit his own ends. His was the master mind that held an unbalanced economic structure in the semblance of equilibrium. Acting like some catalytic agent, it bound antagonistic social groups together in a faithless society, like chemical elements in an unstable mixture.

He lived the autocrat of a realm founded on the dominance of gold. Proprietor of billions of wealth, surrounded by a court of rapacious financiers struggling for his favor, he was also the target of countless plots that challenged his supremacy. The organization he ruled reached a finger into every department of government, every branch of industry, and taught the single lesson that disobedience meant ruin, treachery, death.

"Let me present Dr. Edgerton," said Manse, "member for many years of the faculty of the University of Chicago."

Vivian Ransler acknowledged the introduction coolly, shifting her eyes only for an instant from Jimmy, who added, "I am James Manse, master of arts and science, a student."

"Both unemployed?" she asked.

"Certainly," answered the doctor. "Why otherwise should we have been where we could do you a service?"

She smiled brilliantly, and looked at the speaker with more marked interest.

"I thought," she explained, "that only educated pacifists slept on the Oak Street beach. I was dared to go down the stairs alone and watch them wake up and scramble for shelter when the storm hit them."

She laughed, and carelessly signed the voucher form the guard presented. At the same instant a peal of thunder accompanied a scattering downfall of big raindrops.

"You're coming home with me for breakfast," she declared. "My father owes you thanks. We must hurry or we'll get wet."

Allowing no time for consideration of an invitation that carried the flavor of royal command, she led them to a glistening limousine standing at the nearby curb.

"You, Mr. Manse, shall sit beside me," she directed. "It will be a bit crowded, because there's another passenger in the car already."

An attendant jumped down from a reversed rumble seat where, armed with a short machine gun, he guarded the wake of the limousine against too close proximity of suspicious vehicles. As he opened the door, an electric light inside blazed up, exposing a disheveled young man in evening clothes, slumped in one corner of the back seat asleep.

"My escort," said Vivian Ransler with scorn. "Drunk and rather disorderly."

She seated herself beside him. Jimmy sat next to her in the other corner. Doctor Edgerton took the seat unfolded in front of them. The door closed, and the light went out. A moment later the car was gliding northward along the upper drive.

Small searchlights in recesses cut in the curb stone at the street level threw out fans of electric radiance that made the boulevard light as day, in spite of the darkness above.

On the commodius back seat it seemed to Jimmy that he was crowded more than necessary. At hip and shoulder he felt the warm pressure of the woman next to him. A pleasant heat spread through his veins.

The storm burst in fury, with roars of thunder and swirls of driving rain. Jimmy pictured to himself the rush of his recent fellow beachcombers to shelter under the drive, where contacts with the roughest element of Lower Level population were always imminent and dangerous, except in broad day.

Regardless of the downpour, the car shot ahead for several miles before it slackened speed, turned to the left toward one of the palaces of the far north side, and stopped. A light flashed upon the chauffeur to identify him. Immediately a ponderous steel door rose like a curtain, allowing the car to drive into a stone box-court.

Ransler Castle, like many such modern structures, built of golden-yellow glassite reinforced with steel, rose a dozen stories above the level of the upper drive. The only entrances to the splendid living equipment of its owner were from the court in which the limousine stopped. The curtain of steel slid down behind it.

An attendant opened the door of the car. Manse alighted, and offered his hand to Vivian Ransler. She took it with pronounced pressure. As Dr. Edgerton got out, she addressed the chauffeur concerning her drunken escort.

"Take Mr. Braxley away, Pierre," she said, curtly.

Jimmy noticed several erect, quietly dressed men, standing about the brilliantly lighted court, apparently oblivious of himself and Dr. Edgerton. He needed no assurance to be certain that they were members of the Ransler Protective Corps, some of whom were on duty day and night, alert detectives suspecting bombs in innocent packages, poisons, persons whose presence was not at once self-explanatory.

Vivian Ransler led the way up half a dozen broad steps to a magnificently designed doorway. The door itself, a masterpiece of bas-relief, swung open before them. They entered a hall spacious enough for a public building.

"Call Thompson," the girl ordered the doorman.

He pulled back a small bronze plaque on the wall, and pressed one of the electric buttons sunk in a niche.

A gray haired, dignified man appeared silently.

"Show these gentlemen to an apartment," she directed. "A relaxing drink will help them to enjoy a few hours' rest. Probably they will not care to breakfast before eleven."

She looked at Manse, raising her eyebrows enquiringly; and when he bowed assent, added, "Any time after that at their convenience. They are in your care, Thompson."

The valet bowed low.

"Good night," concluded Vivian Ransler imperiously.

CHAPTER TWO

WHEN Jimmy Manse awoke amid the lavish hospitality of Ransler Castle it was not yet eleven o'clock. Out of a jumbled dream his perception of reality struggled to extricate itself. At the same time his brain strove to reproduce fantastic picture-experiences subconsciously painted while he slept.

The most vivid of these represented himself laboriously climbing a high ladder out of a pool of gesticulating humanity. Men and women cursed him and tried to drag him back. He kicked off clutches at his legs, stamped upon hands that grasped the rungs at his feet.

He would not look down into the dark confusion, but held his gaze persistently upward into a golden effulgence emanating from a lascivious goddess, who kept beckoning him to follow her. Above the vile language of the mob he heard a clear, girlish voice calling over and over again, like a soul in distress:

"Jimmy, don't go!"

That part of the dream echoed and re-echoed in his memory as he opened his eyes wide, stretched out luxuriously in the soft bed and wrinkled his forehead at the aluminum ceiling traced with curious arabesques inlaid in black.

His gaze wandered to the walls that seemed incredibly distant, to the tessellated floor of rough surfaced metal tiles in black and silver, over which lay scattered in meticulous carelessness thick, crumpling rugs of camel's hair, dyed in light shades of green, with angular designs worked on them in black.

Hunching himself higher on the pillows, he noticed the electric clock in the frosted silver footboard, realized he was wide awake, and that it was eight minutes of eleven.

He threw back the covering and swung his legs over the bedside. His bare feet met carefully placed bath sandals, and settled into them comfortably. For an instant he looked down admiringly at his dark green, silk pajamas, provided by the valet who had showed him and Doctor Edgerton to adjoining rooms. Then he quickly flipped a fleecy robe over his shoulders, crossed to one of the tall, narrow windows, raised the curtain and pressed a spring that split the flat pane into broad open slats of glass.

A summer breeze drifted in from the lake, which appeared from his tenth-story outlook surprisingly close. Long since the rain had ceased. The storm had passed over. The sky was cloudless. A perfect Fourth of July to commemorate the noble Declaration of Independence!

When Jimmy entered the bathroom he found it a broad corridor of Roman splendor. On the green marble floor strips of darker green cork matting led like paths among urns of flowering plants to machines for athletic exercise, to heat cabinets, light baths, couches.

Lounging chairs offered silent invitation to relax. Of various shapes they stood at irregular intervals along the rim of a swimming pool of bright water, through which brilliant sunshine, pouring down from windows high up near the ceiling, set wavy lines of refracted light dancing on the tiled sides beneath the surface.

An attendant laid down a book, rose quickly and bade Jimmy good morning. He was naked save for shorts and sandals—a man of fifty with the muscular arms and barrel chest of an ancient gladiator. The book he had been reading, Jimmy noted while dropping off robe and pajamas, was Aeschylus' "Agamemnon," in the original text.

Jimmy wallowed in clouds of steam in the glass steam room, enjoyed the stimulation of a cool shower, and leisurely descended into the pool. When he climbed out, the attendant wrapped him in a warm, rough towel, and led him to a white rubber-cushioned, marble slab for a comforting massage.

"Doctor Edgerton is already up," the man said as he kneaded Jimmy's vertebrae with the accurate facility of an osteopath. "A remarkable scholar, sir, although he depreciates the value of proficiency in the classics."

"He does that sometimes," grunted Jimmy. "Tell me—" he hesitated for an appelation.

"Brown," supplied the attendant. "Brown, sir. Harvard '24. Number three on the crew for two years, and stroke as a senior. Doctor's degree in 2027. For the last ten years attached to the city household of Mr. Ransler in the present capacity."

He knuckled Jimmy's spine with additional pressure and added, "I've always stuck to Greek and Latin—particularly research into the psychological functions of the chorus in Greek tragedy. Please turn over, sir."

Jimmy rolled over on his back.

"Wouldn't mathematics or science be more satisfying?"

"So Thompson contends," replied Brown, "*but de gustibus non est disputandum.* You recall Thompson, sir? Our chief valet. Yale '23. Valedictorian of his class. A powerful mind. He presented an excellent paper on four-dimensional space at the last meeting of our Household Club."

"What's that?" asked Jimmy, as he sat up on the edge of the marble slab.

"The Ransler Household Employees' Association—two hundred and forty members. We flatter ourselves it not incapably diffuses higher education on the Upper Level. The most menial scullion in the Ransler kitchen has had the advantages of at least a year or two of postgraduate work in one of the better universities. Your gown, sir."

Jimmy slipped into the thick Turkish bath gown Brown held for him.

"Dr. Edgerton expects you, sir," suggested the man opening a door through which Jimmy passed into a large octagonal bedroom, twin to his own.

"Come in, James," greeted the professor buoyantly. "Help me pick out a shirt and a necktie, and choose one for you, too. Thompson tells me we'll be measured for clothes shortly, and provided with other accouterments for a fitting presentation to Mr. Ransler."

He was inspecting a display of underwear, hose, and linen spread out on a vehicle like a large tea cart, while Thompson with deft unobtrusiveness influenced the selection.

"I don't get the necessity for all this," objected Jimmy. "I feel—"

"My boy," interrupted the doctor, "forget that this is the Fourth of July. Accept as wisdom imitation of the Romans when you're in Rome."

To the valet he continued smoothly, "Thompson, I have every confidence in your understanding and taste concerning what is requisite for gentlemen who find themselves in the position of Mr. Manse and me. I give you carte blanche to provide what is appropriate for both of us."

"Thank you, sir," murmured Thompson. "Your breakfast will be served at once, sir. Here is a pleasant little sunroom that has the atmosphere of complete privacy."

They entered a glass-enclosed nook that offered a breath-taking view north, east and south. In the background spread out the lake. Directly below stretched the boulevard with its palaces and villas, cursed and envied, hated and worshiped, by the millions of underpaid workers and the unemployed on the Lower Level.

Dr. Edgerton motioned Jimmy toward a chair at a little table upon which two places glistened with crystal goblets and silver against the sheen of white damask.

"Behold!" he cried, looking out at the vista of thrilling architecture and streaming motor cars. "The Gold Coast is at our feet. This is a moment of the marvelous—a culmination in the mysterious concatenation of events wherein the effect of observed causes has been unforeseen. A fortuitous incident squeezes the technique of our lives into a new pattern of habits."

"I don't follow you, doctor," Jimmy opposed with some bitterness. "This taste of splendid living will linger to poison our old life when we go back to it."

"Why prophesy so miserable a reaction?" exclaimed the professor. "Why not look to survival among these new surroundings? The man whose hospitality we now accept was once a brutal outlaw in the darkest places of the Lower Level."

A discreet knock sounded as prelude to the entrance of an alert young man with a small brief-case, followed by a butler who served grapefruit juice, well flavored with Santa Cruz rum, in exquisitely plain, tall, golden cups.

"I am one of the house secretaries," the young man announced. "I'm instructed to inform you that multiplicity of affairs so crowd Mr. Ransler's time that he cannot grant you an interview until tomorrow. Meanwhile you are to consider this your home."

Tactfully he made them aware that the etiquette of Ransler Castle prescribed the entertainment of guests in seclusion, pending formal recognition of their presence by their host.

He opened his brief case and produced two envelopes, while the butler was removing the golden cups from which Jimmy and the professor had drunk the delicate cocktail.

"I sent for your birth and experience cards from the municipal index," he continued, "and have obtained Upper Level tax-cards which you'll find in these envelopes. Your names have been registered as citizens with full rights."

"Extremely kind," said Jimmy, "but we're causing a lot of trouble."

Brightly the secretary smiled.

"We have no trouble here," he murmured.

"If it will interfere with no plans," Jimmy resumed. "I'll return to the Lower Level this afternoon for a few hours."

"You and Dr. Edgerton are to exercise the utmost freedom in coming and going until your reception by the master. A car will be waiting within an hour."

The secretary laid the two envelopes on the table.

"The tax-cards will secure special attention from guards at all gates to the Lower Level, from members of the Ransler Protective Corps, from Upper Lever municipal officials and employees. On the Lower Level they may be dangerous to show unless a member of our secret service chances to be present."

He rose slowly and added:

"You will find me or one of my colleagues always at hand here and easily summoned. Merely touch the indicated button on the call board in the cabinet at the head of your bed." He bowed and left the room.

When the secretary had withdrawn, Dr. Edgerton looked at Jimmy sharply.

"Why do you want to go back to the Lower Level?" he asked.

The young man's face flushed.

"I promised to see Miriam Estley. She expects me."

The professor gazed at him thoughtfully.

"It is as I supposed," he said with quiet kindness. "My boy, I've told you that in some things I would not attempt to advise you. What I said I meant, but remember that the bright prospects of your future are up here, not down on the Lower Level."

Jimmy rose from the table abruptly. "Let's get dressed," he remarked irrelevantly. "The tailor will be coming shortly to take our measurements."

It was afternoon when they descended in an aluminum elevator to the main floor, where Thompson led them through one of several halls to a side entrance into the court. A small car was waiting.

"To the first exit from the Upper Level in the Lincoln Park area," Jimmy directed the chauffeur.

The Upper Level was six miles wide and extended along the lake shore from Evanston to the Indiana State line. It had a population of about two million.

The car swept southward over the ground-metal, indestructible surface of the drive. Along the broad walk on each side people were returning from the holiday service at the Uptown Temple of Power. Most of them were servants, secretaries, persons in clerical positions, municipal employees representative of the vast majority of Upper Level population. For their livelihood they depended on gigantic corporations, trusts, the whims of hundreds of millionaires vying with one another in the extravagance of their establishments and in the number of their personal attaches and business aids.

The seriousness of the crowd struck Jimmy forcibly. No smiling faces leavened it. These holiday-makers were constrained and formal, as if engrossed in grave duties or treading unfamiliar and perhaps dangerous paths.

Always among the moving throng was a sprinkling of broad shouldered, military-looking men and women, who wore on sleeve or breast some distinctive insignia. They were members of various protective corps—male and female bravos—maintained by the financiers and directors of industry. Highly paid, held to punctilious public behavior by iron discipline, they expected no pardon for a breach of their employer's code or failure to carry out his orders. Carefully chosen from among the uneducated, roughest element of Lower Level society, they were trained in military camps. Out of this class George Ransler had risen like a modern Napoleon.

The importance of a financier might have been gauged by the strength of his corps, if that were known; but it could only be guessed at. It was subject to secret limitation by Ransler himself, absolute monarch in a private feudal system underlying the forms of democratic government. He exacted financial fealty from every leader of industry, every merchant prince, every money baron within the scope of domination he had ruthlessly extended during a score of years, and now struggled to maintain at the peak of its efficiency.

Woe to the upstart millionaire in whom some sudden stroke of good fortune destroyed the sense of financial relativity. Did he but reach out for power beyond the limits set by the master mind, his doom was preordained. Fortunate for him if he surrendered promptly, and suffered no worse than demotion to insignificance in the world of finance.

Dr. Edgerton turned from the window to his young companion.

"James," he declared, "the most powerful man in the world considers himself under obligation to us. If we're wise, our future is assured."

"Absurd!" retorted Jimmy.

"You don't understand," sighed the professor. "This is the center of the Ransler octopus of dominion. Here is the brain; elsewhere throughout the country are only tentacles directed from afar. Secret forces are always merging to strike at the master unawares. Financial interests, ostensibly allied to support his policies, are always plotting his downfall. Such a man magnifies a favor done him by a stranger, and punishes to the last extremity even a friend's innocent interference with his plans. It cannot be otherwise within the range of human nature."

The car came to a stop at the gate two blocks south of where Diversey Boulevard branched westward from the Lake Shore Drive. Dr. Edgerton and Jimmy alighted and showed their tax-cards to the guard, who copied the identifying numbers to be instantly transmitted by typograph to every exit from the Upper Level in order to record their absence.

They descended the narrow stairway, and halted to part company.

"See Miriam Estley and tell her your adventure," said the doctor. "I shall visit the grand plaza in the park. Thousands of the educated proletariat are gathering there to hear patriotic oratory. You will find me on the outskirts of the crowd near the lower drive; or," he added smiling, "at the Zoo close by, for I can never long contemplate free human beings in mass without becoming eager to study wild beasts in captivity."

CHAPTER THREE

THE Lower Level reached out far beyond the western edge of the upper plain. Its population, according to the 2048 municipal census, included 7,683,704 persons above the age of twelve. More than half of them were unemployed, or students earning a pittance by helping the horde of city employees.

This lower region was divided into two hundred and fifty municipal sections, each a mile square. Every ten of these formed a community provided with at least one free lodging-house, one free restaurant, one free theater; and lecture rooms in which educators conducted free university extension courses at all hours of the day and night.

Residential buildings under municipal control furnished housing at rentals fixed by city ordinance. It was possible to obtain an apartment rent free, if the applicant could attest by examination a required proficiency in general education, science or art.

In such an apartment in the art colony of the Ninety-fourth Section lived Miriam Estley. She was a "Daughter of the City," one of the thousands brought up from infancy in municipal institutions.

All records of the parentage of these civic children were destroyed, and up to the age of five they were continually shifted from one institution to another, so as to eradicate every trace of their identity. After being equalized in this manner each of them received from the Bureau of Nomenclature a name, which appeared as the first entry on an individual experience chart, kept in the Municipal Index as a public record until "death or disappearance."

Although the number of children reared by their own parents dwindled rapidly, the birth rate did not decrease commensurately. Nor were drastic laws to enforce observance of birth control so effective as had been predicted. Increasing unemployment met no offsetting decline in population.

At the door of Miriam Estley's studio Jimmy touched the electric bell, and glanced into the little oval recorder of the vision-scope, so that she might see who her caller was without being seen.

The door opened immediately.

"You're late, Jimmy boy," she smiled in greeting.

" 'Clocks are slave drivers against who we should revolt.' " he quoted gaily.

"But time is all we have, just the same," she retorted.

A serious vein in her joyous personality intimated a sense of responsibility far beyond her years.

She was a lovely girl, not more than twenty, in a loose Russian blouse caught up by a buckle on each side over the hip, and many-pleated short skirt, she had the trimness of a young soldier. Her clipped hair revealed pink, little ears against a small head. She looked at Jimmy out of dark eyes, wide apart above a straight nose with delicate nostrils. Her smiling mouth was both firm and tender.

"My fortune's made!" cried Jimmy with enthusiasm, "or at least it's in the making, if Dr. Edgerton knows what he's talking about. I'm not sure he does, but it isn't hard for me to believe him."

"Sit down here, Jimmy, and tell me all about it."

She made room for him by removing from a chair to the floor a drawing-board with a half finished sketch tacked on it. In the rather bare little room, a skylight looking to the north took the place of one entire wall. On the others a few drawings, and on an easel some work in color, broke the monotony of a grey background.

Jimmy narrated the adventure that had gained for himself and Dr. Edgerton foothold on the Upper Level.

"Perfectly gasping!" she exclaimed. "Just think of that old professor fighting like a medieval swordsman, and holding the stairs like Horatius at the bridge."

"What about me, Mirry? Can't you see me rescuing the beautiful lady who's going to get her father to make me president of a bank or something, so that you and I can live happily ever after?"

"I don't like the lady, Jimmy. I don't think she's nice. She's a vampire. I've heard ghastly stories about her."

"Don't believe 'em. It isn't necessary."

"I won't, Jimmy boy, but don't you let the luxury of the Upper Level corrupt you."

"How can it when I carry a declaration of marriage in my pocket, waiting for you to sign the moment you will consent? It seems like a pledge of troth, and it's much less conspicuous than your glove would be pinned on my shoulder."

"That's perfectly gorgeous," she laughed, and added seriously, "we can wait until I get a picture accepted by the Municipal Academy and you get a position with the Bureau of Architecture. We're not the same as these excessively free people all around us who mate like stupid animals. For you and me the state can never reduce love to physiology. The greatest freedom is born of control; the greatest love, of faith."

"When you're so serious you're very wonderful to look at, Miriam. I'd like to see you talk about love with my friend Dr. Edgerton."

"Don't be silly," she replied quickly. "I'm not highly educated. I wouldn't know how to answer him when he tried to tell me that love is just a chemical affinity that sometimes causes dangerous explosions. If that's all love is, I'm glad I don't know it."

"Most people like that kind of talk."

"The poorest artist knows better. And so do you. Don't let that old professor make you think the way he does."

It was three o'clock when Jimmy left the little studio to rejoin Dr. Edgerton. He found him on the outskirts of a mass meeting of the educated unemployed, who sat in groups on the grass, or moved about restlessly. Amplifiers drenched every spot of the plaza with the oratory of flamboyant speakers, making extravagant proposals for improving social and economic conditions.

Professor Willys W. Dormer declared that the public suicide chambers ought to be closed. Although these provided means for taking one's own life instantly by a single inhalation of death gas, the number of suicides had dropped sharply since access to the gas chambers had been made free. Professor Dormer urged the passage of a law prohibiting suicide and fixing a severe penalty for attempting it. This, he contended, would so increase it that the general death rate would rise sufficiently to relieve the economic pressure of unemployment.

Dr. Stanilaus Zerner, eminent pathologist, urged the establishment of free brothels. These he asserted would destroy the opportunity for sin to earn decent wages, and improve the public health and morals.

Professor Edgard Merenski, noted pacifist, proposed abrogation of the law of self-defense. In his opinion such an attitude on the part of the state would put an end to crimes of violence.

These suggestions elicited earnest attention from most of the hearers. Their mass-educated minds, jaded by the new ideas advanced in academic theses on social and economic improvement, sought to apply only tenets of formal logic to all proposals.

Dr. Edgerton seized Jimmy's arm.

"Let's get away from this. I want to talk to you where we can't be overheard."

The young man accompanied him under the upper drive to a spot of isolation on the beach, out of earshot of sprawlers in the sand, who tried to nap, or aimlessly tossed pebbles into the water.

Affecting the most casual air, the professor addressed Jimmy with intense earnestness.

"I've been under surveillance all afternoon," he said in a low voice. "The man watching me has just squatted down in the sand a few yards away. Don't look."

"No one has been following me," replied Jimmy.

"One man must have been detailed to watch us both. When we separated he had to choose whom to follow; and he chose me."

"Why should we be spied upon?" exclaimed Jimmy with heat.

"Tut! Tut!" cautioned the doctor. "We've been thrust into a world new to us—a world alive with power and throbbing with conflicting forces."

"But Ransler is supreme."

"So we suppose. But do we know what is going on beneath the surface of a life we've only glimpsed? What we do know is that one who rises to citizenship on the Upper Level is never cast down again. He remains a citizen until he dies or disappears."

Jimmy fingered his jaw thoughtfully.

"Let me tell you something else," continued the professor. "The meetings of the people in all sections of the Lower Level today are being used for some deeper purpose than celebrating the Fourth of July."

"Nothing in the oratory we just listened to would give any such indication," objected Jimmy.

"Bah!" returned the professor. "The persons in the park and here on this beach are educated proletariat. Demosthenes and Cicero combined couldn't stir them to action. The springs of audacity within them are dried up. It's the ignorant who are being aroused—by fear!"

"Fear of what?"

"Propagandists are whispering among them that plants, factories, whole sections of industrial communities are being mined by order of Ransler, and will be blown up with tremendous loss of life to create reconstruction work and reduce the number of the unemployed."

"Unthinkable!" cried Jimmy.

"You might believe it if you worked in a crowded shop three hours a day, and knew that secret tunnels controlled by Ransler honeycombed the ground beneath your feet."

Jimmy was silent a moment. Then he asked:

"What ought we to do?"

"Nothing," answered the professor. "When we return to the Upper Level it's for us to forget the troubles and miserable futility of the life down here."

They strolled to the stairs, ascended and showed their tax-cards through a wicket to the guard.

Out on the upper drive the professor drew a long breath of relief.

"The very atmosphere up here is exhilarating," he ejaculated. "One gets above the pall of confused, aimless thought, the spiritless waiting day after day, the mental sickness vaunting a freedom that smothers any possible methodical effort."

When they got back to their luxurious quarters they found dinner clothes laid out for them. Promptly they took off their old clothing and allowed Thompson to carry it way for incineration. This seemed like burning the last bridge. The spirits of the doctor rose accordingly, but Jimmy felt depressed. He dropped into an easy chair in the doctor's room, his mind filled with thoughts of Miriam.

Dr. Edgerton gazed at him searchingly.

"Less than twenty-four hours ago," he said briskly, "you vowed you would rise to the Upper Level. Well, here you are. You ought to feel uplifted."

But Jimmy was thinking of a big industrial plant in the Ninety-fourth Section, close to the art colony. He wondered whether it stood above charges of explosive, ready to rend it into ruin at the touch of a button in some secret office on the Upper Level.

"My father got up here, too," he said listlessly.

"You told me he was a chemist, but that's all," rejoined the doctor.

"He made a discovery of some kind. It was going to revolutionize the world he told my mother—save mankind from the self-destruction toward which he thought progressive civilization was carrying us."

"Something of a visionary?" suggested the doctor looking at him sympathetically.

"I hardly remember him. When he left us to come up here he promised to return and get us; but he never did."

The doctor showed surprise.

"Is he a citizen of the Upper Level now?" he asked.

"I don't know where he is. Dead, I suppose. Almost immediately after being admitted to the full rights of citizenship, he disappeared. From then until my mother died, we lived on a pension."

"From the municipality?"

"The city paid it as trustee. We never could find out its source." He scratched his head thoughtfully and added, "There ought to be some record that tells what became of him, and why we got the pension."

"Don't pry into that," admonished the doctor. "Restrain what might turn out to be unseemly inquisitiveness. Be patient. Learn by listening what proper questions are."

He fumbled at the radio panel on which numerous golden knobs were arranged above plates labeled "Art," "Music," "Lectures," "Drama," and so on.

"For the first time," he remarked, "we have a chance to hear exclusive broadcasts on wave lengths impossible of reception on the Lower Level."

He turned the "News" knob, which cut abruptly into a recital of disjointed paragraphs. A colorless voice intoned a brief description of the holiday service at the Uptown Temple of Power. Announcement followed that the air above the Upper Level, except secret channels known only to pilots with special licenses from the Master, had been closed to navigation by net-ray protection.

Dr. Edgerton's interest did not lessen when the voice took up routine items from public offices; the censored police news, dealing chiefly with accidents; the weather forecast, crop conditions.

A moment later came the list of those who that day had disappeared. A vaguely familiar name caught Jimmy's attention. He held up his hand.

"Where did we hear that before?"

"Braxley?" repeated the doctor slowly, trying to remember. "Braxley?"

Jimmy jumped to his feet.

"That's the name of Vivian Ransler's escort in the car last night," he cried.

He was still puzzling over this coincidence when he rolled into bed. As his head sank back, he heard from the soft-speaker in his pillow the soothing strains of a Violin, played with the delicate skill of a virtuoso.

The low notes began to sound exactly like a human voice. And then he realized that they had, indeed, become a human voice of marvelous quality, melodious and inspiring, vibrant with vitality.

"I am ready to fall into delightful slumber," the voice murmured, dreamily. "I have no fretful cares to worry me. I am at perfect ease in mind. I am part of the overwhelming power that rules the Upper Level. My single duty is to help increase the sum total of that power by harmonious acquiescence."

The voice imperceptibly became the soothing strains of a violin again.

Jimmy, on the verge of plunging into slumber, vaguely divined that what he had heard would be repeated again and again all night long while he slept—a subtle hypnosis poured into his subconscious mind.

CHAPTER FOUR

GEORGE RANSLER was the tenth and most autocratic in the line of masters that had ruled the nation since the dreadful Revolution of Despair in the middle of the twentieth century.

The bewildering changes wrought in the social organization had been effected not without bloodshed, but the acts of violence had been in the nature of private crimes rather than the result of public uprising. In this respect the revolution stood out unique in the annals of mankind. It had not overthrown the form of government.

Under the old capitalists the decline of employment, buying power, business activity, that began in 1929, went on to the bitter end with only spasmodic interruptions, the worst of which was the hectic period of mad inflation and gambling that burst out in 1940. Bankers and industrial leaders continued to betray the absurd confidence of the people. They sacked private and public treasuries like licensed vandals.

The very surpluses of business entities made the ultimate plunge into bottomless depression impossible to halt. In numerous fields big corporations continued to operate long after possibility of making a profit had vanished. Where there was only business enough for one or two, half a dozen fought for it, and all suffered heavy loss.

This senseless policy corporate officials upheld without a dissenting voice. So long as they could keep the corporations going, their salaries were assured. At the same time they were able through the machinations of short-selling in the stock market to divest themselves of their own shares, while keeping their names on corporate records as large stockholders.

They took great credit for effecting economies in management. These they achieved by the simple expedient of reducing the number of workers and cutting the wages of those who remained.

This process continued for years after it was clear that the only way toward recovery lay in restricting the number of corporations so as to make capacity of output fit reasonable expectancy of demand, in order that production in every industry might once more be gainful instead of disastrous.

Those few observers who expounded this common sense, the press and public alike hooted with derision. Popular slogans of the day urged pretense that no depression existed and steadfast confidence in the capitalists whose treacherous leadership had brought on the breakdown and was daily making matters worse.

Everyone perceived that much of the economic trouble grew out of replacement of human labor by machinery, but no attempt was made to restrict the number of hours machines might run. Instead, endless discussion went on about the advisability of reducing the number of hours allowed for human labor, with commensurate reduction in wages.

Finally the corporations were drained of their funds and could borrow no more from the depleted national treasury. The number of persons on federal, state and civic doles rose above thirty million.

Then the capitalists began to retire from their positions of trust and responsibility. They easily shouldered their burdens on to younger men who thought opportunity still offered to glean something from the wreckage.

Corrupt judges, lawyers, and financiers formed rings and divided among themselves exorbitant fees garnered from receiverships and bankruptcy proceedings—sweet carrion of industry. The creditors got nothing.

By 1950 the sad result of nearly two centuries of national economic life was a vast shell of prosperity that contained nothing within it but the rotten fruit of human rapacity.

Had it not been for highly organized bands of criminals of a low order the nation inevitably would have disintegrated into barbarism.

The old capitalists had piled up secret hoards of gold upon which they counted to establish themselves abroad, if flight seemed advisable. But their contemplated emigration became too dangerous. Foreign countries grew more unsafe for rich Americans than the home land they had ravished. Here they were able to buy protection from leaders of the criminal bands that were beginning to usurp the powers of government.

Those bands grew bolder and stronger. They merged into fewer and larger associations that fought among themselves for supremacy. The gold in banks and the hoards of private persons became the object and sinews of their warfare. When one band defeated another it plundered the capitalists who paid the latter for protection.

Torture of millionaires to make them divulge the location of caches of gold became an almost daily occurrence. Many of the victims resisted with the most heroic fortitude. It was not uncommon for a millionaire to allow himself to be murdered by inches rather than give up the hidden gold he had looted during his respectable career in industry or finance.

The ultimate outcome was inevitable. Gradually the old capitalists were stripped of their gold. The criminal bands became associated in a single system. Their energetic leaders, like the pirates, soldiers of fortune, and robber barons of the Middle Ages, having obtained the upper hand by violence, and most of the gold supply by murder and theft, founded a new aristocracy that differentiated itself from the masses into the ruling class.

The most capable of the old industrialists and the most astute of the old financiers, no longer dangerous because beyond the prime of life and reduced to helpless poverty, were given employment at insignificant wages by the System, which now began to reorganize industry.

Reconstruction was pushed forward with the simple directness of despotic control. Creditors were ordered to consider debts due them canceled, and to deliver at once to the System all bonds and shares of stock in their possession. This they did with promptitude, for failure to comply meant speedy punishment.

The masses of unemployed and the workers looked upon these developments as the dawn of a new freedom. The System fostered this belief and provided more free educational facilities, better free lodgings, free food, free amusements; and imitated the jargon of science in promising a future when everyone who wished to work would be able to earn at least twenty thousand dollars a year by employing himself a few hours a day.

Promulgation of plans for gigantic improvements convinced the public that this goal could be attained. Construction of the Upper Level boulevards began. Funds for this and other supposed public works, carried on under concessions from various branches of government, were provided by the System, which acquired the right to levy taxes by paying fixed sums for this privilege.

As the work progressed, cash for labor and materials was easily raised by financial operations founded on the same scheme that the old capitalists had employed: the making of pieces of paper, called securities, exchangeable at their market price for gold.

Financial centralization attained an intensity of focus never before dreamed possible. No domestic corporation was independent of the System, which built up and maintained confidence in all issues of stocks and bonds by its absolute control of the gold supply.

In all American cities foreign quarters disappeared. Unknown persons who spoke with a foreign accent were subject to arrest and deportation if they could not satisfactorily account for their residence in the United States.

In most of Europe the large cities were mere oases of civilization in deserts of anarchy. Sporadic civil warfare went on continuously. To the riffraff of the old world, murderers, thieves, degenerates of all kinds, the United States looked like a heaven for malefactors.

Rigid laws prohibiting immigration did not prevent infiltration of foreigners from countries where social and economic conditions were terrible beyond description. Foreign schools, with instructors who taught proficiency in colloquial American, enabled graduates successfully to pose as citizens of this country, if they could once get into it. Smuggling in aliens was a profitable business of criminal gangs on the Lower Level.

The powers of governing prescribed by the Federal Constitution were vitiated under scholastic interpretations of the Supreme Court into a mere ritual. The dictum of the most learned judicial minds held that pretense of respect for the law was more *pro bono publico* than effort to enforce it, which might arouse sedition. Government as a whole degenerated into the feeble lassitude in which Christianity had long been sunk.

The courts principally occupied themselves with procedure designed to establish new precedents that would give to modern economic activities with a criminal aspect the substance of legality. Public thought inclined toward the repeal of all statutes, an idea popular with the masses on the Lower Level, who continued to suppose that abrogation of law meant greater liberty.

Already they were surfeited with a spurious freedom; but they did not know it. Exempt from direct taxation they failed to perceive that this immunity from cost of government was no more than a badge of servitude, or I the mark of a savage in a new land. It was not a willing grant from a generous government, but merely the outcome of stern necessity.

Low wages and widespread unemployment had made collection of taxes from the masses impossible long before invisible private management presumed to direct the machinery of the state.

To rising generations on the Lower Level the most inviting opportunity for advancement seemed to lie in higher education. The student, moreover, could sustain his self-respect by considering himself engaged in dignified effort to carry forward the accumulating knowledge of mankind.

But the aristocracy on the Upper Level—made up of descendants of the criminal saviors of the nation, and new members who had sufficient daring and vitality to fight their way up from the roughest element of the Lower Level—held no such view. They partook of education sparingly.

Although before the revolution the country had been overridden by an academic priesthood of professors, doctors, instructors, lecturers, teachers, educators of all sorts, and expenditures for public education had mounted to more than two-thirds of the entire cost of government, the criminal leaders in no way interfered with free schooling. On the contrary, they gradually took over the whole scheme of educating the masses and expanded it to the utmost.

Education was free as air, from the primary school to the most advanced postgraduate work in the greatest university; but the pay of educators was reduced to a pittance. They were led to believe, however, that it would become more liberal at some future time. Many of them finally did receive generous emolument, but almost invariably they died or disappeared shortly thereafter.

The favorable attitude toward diffusion of learning was due to the keen foresight of the first master. He perceived that educational training ironed out of most untutored minds the force of originality that gave birth to thoughts of revolt.

This master ordered to be carved on a golden panel in one of the conference rooms of the System, where it still remained, a quotation from Schopenhauer, gloomy philosopher of the nineteenth century, brought to his attention by his faithful bootblack, an elderly man of great erudition, president emeritus of a famous eastern center of learning.

This quotation read:

"Scholarship makes most men more unintelligent and stupid than they are by nature."

Possibility of themselves harvesting these desiccated fruits of scholarship the ruling class sedulously avoided; but they made use of scholarship in others with the utmost shrewdness. Every scientific worker who gained distinction in the laboratories of educational institutions immediately received an offer to go to work at handsome remuneration in a private laboratory of the System.

The humanizing of prisons progressed to the noblest extreme. The penitentiaries, regarded as part of the educational system, took as their models the universities. The appointments were hygienic and artistic.

Every cell was equipped with a private bath. Some had a small study attached with several windows, in which the white enameled bars were arranged in pleasing designs. These quarters were for the worst criminals, most in need of softening influences.

The majority of the inmates came from the Lower Level population, men and women convicted of crimes of violence, the immediate cause of which was almost invariably sex relations.

In Upper Level society the only crimes considered heinous were overt acts against the System itself, or against the sanctity of property. No specific laws defined what these crimes were, and seldom were they tried in the courts. They were punished secretly by the power of the System, directed by the Master. The blows fell like thunderbolts, but left no trace.

At the beginning of the year 2050 the people venerated the Colonial Fathers as deeply as ever, still honored the memory of patriots who had filled the presidential chair, took off their hats when the flag passed by, and revered the Constitution. But the country was a democracy in name only. The form alone remained, a thin disguise for dictatorial rule centered in the Master.

The social organization had reached a development beyond the wildest aspirations of the old capitalists before the Revolution of Despair. An intelligence service supplied the Master every twenty-four hours with up-to-the-minute data on operation of the invisible government. Every morning he received a comprehensive report that was a masterpiece of cooperative brevity. No less than five thousand expurgators, working at night, had a hand in compiling it.

Expert investigators dictated their notes on phonograph disks of uniform size. These went to the chiefs of political, social, and business zones. Each compressed the subject matter that came to him into the compass of a single disk.

This process continued through the medium of branch managers, department heads, group executives, to a deliberative committee of five who prepared the final report, restricted to a budget of precise information and comment that could be heard in one hour's time. The disks recording this were set in an annunciator for the Master to listen to at his convenience.

Every disk that played a part in each daily report was indexed and filed. Thus the Master was always able to obtain at a moment's notice amplification of the smallest hint or detail by applying to the Bureau of Private References.

Besides this service he had a personal corps of hundreds of secret agents, none of whom knew who the others were, continually delving into private life on the Upper Level and the Lower Level for signs of dangerous discontent.

Nevertheless intrigue to forward selfish interests eager for more wealth went on unabated. It had increased as George Ransler, now sixty, grew older. His reign as Master had lasted twenty-three years—much longer than any of the turbulent regimes of his predecessors.

Fearful conjectures of what might follow his sudden death or disappearance welled up unbidden in the public mind.

CHAPTER FIVE

THE System office building filled a whole block in the heart of the financial district. Rising upon hardened steel foundations, thicker than a fortification and sunk to a depth of several hundred feet below the surface of the Lower Level, it towered ninety five stories high.

The mammoth Central Bank occupied the entire main floor on the Upper Level, above impregnable vaults that hugged billions of gold in bars and coin.

In underground fastnesses scientists strove in hidden laboratories to push their research into the closest privacy of nature. Chemists, who knew secrets withheld from a world not yet prepared to hear them, passed their lives in forced seclusion. They toiled on to improve economic conditions that steadily got worse.

The public health grew better. Mortality declined. Longevity increased. But machinery continued to lessen demand for human labor, and make earning a living more and more difficult for the masses.

Bromwell, the secretary who had obtained tax-cards for the doctor and Jimmy, conducted them into the glittering offices of the great banking and brokerage firm of Warrington and Warrington on the second floor. This, like the Central Bank, was a Ransler implement for manipulating vast enterprises to hold the loose fabric of society together.

In the crowded customers' room quotations from markets all over the world clicked and flickered on tall, broad recording boards. Opportunity offered to speculate in every form of security, every commodity; but the Ransler stocks held the focus of attention.

These were shares in clusters of affiliated corporations spoken of with awe as the "Steel Trust," the "Food Trust," the "Transportation Trust," the "Amusement Trust," the "Clothing Trust," and so on interminably. On the industries they represented depended the meager earnings of millions on the Lower Level. As prices of these shares rose or fell, all seemed well with the world, or chaos seemed to threaten.

The secretary excused himself to make their presence known. When he returned he ushered them into a small elevator that shot up to the ninetieth floor. This and the five floors above were the exclusive domain of Ransler and scores of multimillionaires, managers, secretaries, clerks, who formed the inner circle from which issued the directions and commands of the Master.

No higher degree of efficiency could be planned, it seemed to Dr. Edgerton and Jimmy, than characterized by the conduct of the Ransler coordinated business and financial activities.

They emerged from the elevator to find themselves in an ante-room, where a middle-aged man in closely buttoned, tight-fitting coat, that allowed no slack for pockets, awaited them.

"Undoubtedly you are aware," he intimated politely, "that every precaution is taken to obviate endangering the Master's health. Knowing this you will accept as wisdom the request that you change into the prophylactic costume worn by those he accords an audience for the first time."

He pointed to garments laid out on a table.

The doctor smiled at this courteous cunning to search a questionable visitor for weapon, bomb or poison.

He and Jimmy removed their outer clothing, and each put on a garment like an air-pilot's dress, except that the sleeves terminated in gloves and the legs in covering for the feet. They entered the reception room alone.

At the far end George Ransler sat behind a flat desk equipped with intricate appliances for quick communication. He was listening through a telephonic device—attached to the back of his chair—that thrust forward funneled speakers in proximity to his ears. On each side of him a young man watched his every move.

He looked up with weary eyes, cold as ice.

As the callers hesitated inside the door, which automatically locked behind them, he rose and came forward with the vigorous step of a man of forty.

But his face was old and scarred with experience. His massive head hung forward as if too heavy for his hulking shoulders. The bony spareness of his body emphasized ungainly hands and feet.

As he drew near, his presence enveloped the doctor and Jimmy in an aura of subjective influence. A sense of tremendous power overwhelmed them. It held something primitive, ape-like, that connoted soulless force unfit for human personality. But when he spoke his voice was normal, even kindly.

"I am under obligation to you," he began, and held up a restraining hand when the doctor would have made conventional denial.

"At least so I consider myself," he continued, "but not for the reason you suppose. No gallant act has significance, except as it promises latent power for utility. Do you understand me?"

"Perhaps," returned the doctor, softly.

"I require two fresh minds," the Master went on. "One mature, one immature, with which to take clean impressions of transcendent experiments."

A piercing look appraised their fitness.

"Are you satisfied to be the servants of men," he queried, sternly, "or have you the hardihood to serve your race? The first is easy, comfortable and safe; the second, painful and dangerous. I allow you to choose."

Unexpectedly he turned, and strode away to his desk. His fingers formed with lightning swiftness symbols in a sign language. The doctor and Jimmy realized with a shock that the two secretaries were deaf and dumb.

"What unintelligible stuff is this?" whispered Jimmy.

"The truth, perhaps," replied the doctor. "In any event my choice is made."

"And so is mine," added Jimmy excitedly.

The Master returned.

"You have chosen the hazardous course?" he asked.

They nodded gravely.

He motioned them to chairs, and sat down.

"A destructive war for power has begun," he said abruptly. "The Lower Level is alive with propaganda. But the danger is up here. Continental financiers in league with enemies at home plot to gain possession of the gold supply. They are establishing lines of secret communication between the Upper Level and the Lower Level to foment social disturbance below, while they try to wreck financial stability above."

His great head swayed slowly from side to side as he continued rapidly: "They are well aware that our billions of securities and paper money make a wealth that is wholly imaginary. Estimated at hundreds of times the value of the gold supply, it is nevertheless exchangeable for gold on demand. They think that if millions of shares are continuously dumped on the stock market by sellers who demand payment in gold, and hide that gold as fast as they accumulate it, the whole supply can be drained away. Ruin would inevitably follow."

"And," interposed the doctor, "they would have the gold and its unlimited power instead of you."

"In the battle for gold I shall defeat them," declared the Master positively. "But terrific repercussions from such a struggle might tumble the Upper Level down like an earthquake. That's the real peril—destruction of the System!"

His eyes blazed with fanatic fervor.

"The work of my life would be undone," he cried softly, yet with fierce intensity.

A signal, imperceptible to the doctor and Jimmy, caused him to whirl round toward the secretaries, one of whom held up his open hand, palm out. The Master lifted his right hand with forefinger outstretched, and the secretary brought him a message just typed by a noiseless machine on the desk.

At a glance he took in its meaning, and passed it to the doctor and Jimmy.

"A million shares of Steel Preferred," it read, "will be thrown on the market during the last fifteen minutes before the close. Are there instructions?

"C 793."

"A query from a traitor," sneered the Master, with a gesture that caused the second secretary to bring a table and fit its feet upon small plates in the floor in front of them.

In the center of the table dozens of buttons, bearing abbreviations of Ransler stocks, surrounded a square of ground glass. One of these, marked "XX," the Master pressed. The latest quotation of Steel Preferred flashed on the glass in red light. Another quotation and another followed, recording the continuous action of the stock.

Slowly the price began to decline. At intervals it jumped back again spasmodically, but as the minutes passed each recovery regained less of the preceding loss.

The downward trend accelerated until quotations were flashing on the heels of one another in riotous haste. The doctor and Jimmy could imagine the roaring crowd on the floor of the stock exchange, where panic was spreading.

Now and again the Master glanced at the miniature watch set in a ring on a finger of his left hand, but until five minutes before time for the exchange to close he remained unmoved. Then he thrust his arm above his head. The secretaries tapped keys with smart precision.

Almost instantly came the effect. Unlimited buying halted the decline of Steel Preferred. What seemed a rout became a triumph. Up went the price by leaps, until it reached the point at which the break had started. The market closed.

The Master lifted his eyes from the table, and resumed his conversation as if nothing had interrupted it.

"I've allowed you a choice," he told them. "I have taken you into my confidence. The danger is yours. You shall see."

He walked briskly to his desk, and dictated a few incisive sentences into various microphones.

Jimmy felt a wave of depression sweep over him, like a warning that some evil deed impended. The doctor tapped nervously with his foot.

Both experienced a sense of relief when the door through which they had entered opened quietly, and a tall, handsome man came into the room. He looked careworn, but smiled affably.

"Ah, Frederick," cried the Master heartily, "thank you for coming so promptly. My request has not interfered with your plans, I hope."

"Merely a luncheon engagement."

"I wanted you for a little conference here, but I can excuse you."

"Quite unnecessary, sir."

The newcomer, visibly more at ease, looked at the doctor and Jimmy narrowly.

The Master smiled significantly at him.

"These gentlemen are not yet instructed," he said, "so as usual we shall dispense with names till later."

To the doctor and Jimmy he remarked by way of explanation. "It is a pleasant custom of the System to begin every conference of more than three persons, including myself, with a glass of wine. The practice used to be a luncheon, but," he smiled, "busy days put too heavy exercise upon the stomach."

In a corner of the room he opened a wine closet, took a bottle of champagne from a refrigerating compartment, carefully uncorked it and filled four fragile, shining glasses.

"Help me do the honors, Frederick," he called over his shoulder.

The man addressed hurried forward and received two of the glasses of wine. With a curious reluctance in his manner he presented them to the doctor and Jimmy.

The Master approached with the other two glasses. His back had been toward his visitors no more than the fraction of a minute.

To the man he called Frederick he handed one glass, the other he raised toward his own lips, with a stately bow that extended a silent toast to all. He drank slowly, watching over the brim of his glass the three who followed his example.

"I was about to remark when you came in, Frederick," he said pointedly, after a few swallows, "that the first principle of the System is justice—implacable justice that has no pity in it, no sympathy."

Suddenly he glared with a flaming hatred that seemed inhuman, and cried in a terrible voice, "You know the code, Frederick."

The man's jaw dropped.

"I've betrayed no trust," burst from his dry lips.

"Liar," contradicted the Master. "Again today you tried to profit by double-dealing. Now you've executed your own punishment."

The victim stared down at the emptied glass in his hand with terror. It fell to the floor. Swift paralysis from a deadly poison was numbing him. He dropped into a chair, raving protestations that became incoherent and dwindled into silence.

The Master signaled to one of the secretaries.

As the dying man slipped from the chair to the floor, a hidden door opened to admit two hooded figures. Silently they lifted the body, and carried it into the elevator that had brought them up from the labyrinth of chambers and corridors deep beneath the building.

The Master stepped to a microphone.

"To the Librarian of Private References:" he dictated in a voice that did not conceal a note of exultation. "Destroy card C.793, correct coordinating tie-ups; and notify the Municipal Index to withhold announcement that Frederick Augustus Warrington has disappeared."

CHAPTER SIX

THIS cold-blooded retribution, enacted before their eyes, froze Jimmy and the doctor with horror. So visibly did it affect the younger man that Dr. Edgerton, while the Master's back was still turned, pressed a finger on his lips to admonish silence.

He himself presented a calm and resolute countenance when the Master wheeled from the microphone and with no suggestion of remorse in his urbane manner, approached them.

"I will have a mission for you shortly," he promised, intimating that the conference was at an end.

In the ante-room, before Jimmy could say anything, the doctor whispered in his ear with desperate earnestness, "Not a word yet."

Silently they changed back into their own clothing, and descended to the main floor. The secretary who had brought them was nowhere to be seen.

Without speaking, but with the same thought, they hurried eastward on Jackson Boulevard through the early afternoon crowd to Michigan Drive, descended to the Lower Level and sought a spot on the lake front, safe from clandestine listeners.

Quarter of a mile to the southward a throng of the unemployed, massed around the Orpheus Pagoda of amplifiers, listened to the afternoon Bach concert by the Civic Symphony Orchestra.

Jimmy could restrain himself no longer.

"Monstrous!" he burst out in a voice like a sob. "Monstrous! We cannot submit to the hideous designs of such a man."

Dr. Edgerton looked about him cautiously, before replying.

"Consider the situation with more philosophy," he urged with forced coolness. "Our position is of our own choosing. There is no turning back."

"We can refuse to go forward."

Solemnly the doctor shook his head.

"To disobey now might bring upon ourselves the punishment we have just seen inflicted. I have no appetite for suicidal chivalry."

"Nor I for cooperative murder, carried on under the guise of serving humanity."

"My boy," rejoined the doctor kindly, "it is thus that man always carries on service to humanity. The history of his progress is a budget of criminal news; his noblest literature, tales of bloody violence. His primitive gods gloated over bloodshed. He adored them with sacrifices prepared by murder. Newer creeds but gave him the hint to mass production. They demanded sacrifices in larger volume. Millions have been slain over so small a matter as the mode of worshiping the same god."

"You're talking about religious bigotry," interrupted Jimmy.

The doctor answered him patiently. Gods, he pointed out, had always been loaded with responsibility for man's welfare. To be religious was to know some god and imitate him. But as no man could be capable of knowing the real god, each set up his own ideal and made worship of that his religion. The atheist worshiped vacuous fortuity.

In all these millions of ideals one characteristic alone was common—omnipotence. Each man's god was all-powerful, and each man, if opportunity permitted, strove to imitate that quality above all others.

He saw it expressed before his eyes in the operation of nature. By relentless elimination, natural forces sought some inscrutable fitness toward which they drove him onward. The mighty stream of human life rushed into the future through myriad individuals, impermanent ducts through which it gushed into succeeding generations. None of these could have meaning in the fulsome waste of nature, unless it held to an ordained course.

"The individual," he concluded, "is infinitely insignificant, my boy. To nature the only thing important is continuity of the race."

"Do you hold a brief for assassination?" cried Jimmy in disgust.

"I try to explain the truth," replied the doctor. "Assassination has been upheld. The Scriptures applaud when left-handed Ehud, bearing a present to King Eglon, seeks a private conference to deliver a secret message and plunges a dagger, haft and all, into the fat belly of the monarch. And when Jael, succoring the general Sisera fleeing in sore distress, tells him to lie down in her tent and fear not, and then drives a tent peg through his temples while he is fast asleep, and weary.

"Was what we saw today more horrible? Do we know that it registered less necessity in human progress, on the delicate balance that weighs the justice of assassination?"

Jimmy's eyes flashed with scorn.

"Control yourself, my boy," continued the doctor sharply. "Voluntarily we have become the protégés of a dictator equipped with tremendous power, engaged in vast purposes of which we are ignorant. His methods are not our methods."

"He is an unjust tyrant," insisted Jimmy.

The doctor sagely shook his head.

"Who knows what justice is?" he said, calmly. "Here on the Lower Level every resident might contend justice demands that the Upper Level divide its billions of wealth so that everyone has an equal share."

He recalled to Jimmy a story of the ancient Persian King Cyrus, when a boy. One of his schoolfellows had a smock too long; another, a smock too short. The latter was the stronger and forced an exchange. Young Cyrus, acting as judge, decided that because the exchange fitted out both boys better than before, it should stand as if it had been voluntary on both sides.

"And for that decision," Jimmy interposed, "his teacher thrashed him to make him remember that justice forbids taking away what is one's own by force."

"Yes, my boy," the doctor smiled, "but society repeatedly takes away, by force if necessary, what belongs to its members."

"For the good of the mass," countered the young man.

The doctor raised his eyebrows.

The same plea, he said, had been urged to exculpate the assassination of kings, despots, emperors, tyrants, revolutionists, princes, lords, churchmen, presidents, ministers; the slaughter of hundreds of thousands accused of witchcraft; the extermination of believers in one religion by zealots in another.

Perplexity wrinkled Jimmy's forehead.

Justice in nature, the doctor proceeded, was the simple effect of a cause. So the Master regarded it in the vast system he had built up, a living plan driving toward some definite purpose known to him, but not to them. Nothing must hinder its progress. Disloyalty in a human unit was proof of unfitness; a cause that effected its own elimination with the inexorability of impersonal natural law.

"But the punishment is not impersonal," objected the young man.

Dr. Edgerton studied Jimmy's belligerent, youthful face for a moment, and then tried once more to make him understand.

The Master, he said, endeavored to imitate the impersonal precision that was the innate beauty of nature, the essence of all art from the lowest to the highest. It had always been a passion with man, no matter how expressed. The husband of beautiful Madame Recamier could not forego, even on his wedding day, the pleasure of watching the bloody, impersonal precision of the guillotine distributing justice.

A shocking example of sadism, to be sure, but part of the human output of the time, and not unique. In despising cults, their meaning should not be ignored. They might be the seed of mobs; the cultures of revolution.

Assassination itself, he said, took its name from one of them—the Assassins, religious sect that Hassan ben Sabbah founded and shackled into the belief that the orders of their chief proceeded from God himself.

"Is the System of the Upper Level so different?" the doctor asked.

"Would you make the Master a god?" exclaimed Jimmy in contemptuous wonder.

"He has made himself what he is—a godlike attribute—and in his relation to us he exercises the most widely recognized divine characteristic, unlimited power. Bend your mind to reality."

Jimmy looked at Dr. Edgerton with something of the detestation he felt for the Master himself.

"My boy," persisted the doctor kindly, "what profits a noble dead man? Can you not see that justice is only the decision of the greatest power? The surest safety for a man among his fellows lies in the sensitiveness of his adaptability."

"Oh, let me think! Let me think!" cried the boy in a kind of anguish; and he walked away to sit by himself on the trampled sod, worn bare in spots by the aimless feet of the unemployed.

He put his hand in his pocket and touched the declaration of marriage between himself and Miriam that awaited her signature. Sudden longing gripped him so painfully that tears sprang to his eyes.

He called to mind all he knew of her daily life. Little intimate details of their association came back to him with the charm of delightful implication. He saw the determination with which she carried her head, the confidence in her eyes, the beauty of her figure.

He remembered the sturdy simplicity with which she ignored the immature fury of young intellectuals, storming for more freedom. Her quiet merriment at some of their proposals. How she clung to faith in the old idea of chastity, until he had become ashamed of his own acceptance of the prevailing liberality in views concerning sex relations.

No girl was more popular in the group among which they moved, but she maintained her gay modesty unimpaired, and avoided attempts at undesired intimacy by spritely kindness, more effective than anger or disdain. In the circle of her acquaintances with which he was familiar, no one but himself had ever stood on the footing of an accepted lover with the promise of becoming her mate.

What was he to do?

Like an answer came the words of Dr. Edgerton, "Bend your mind to reality."

He rose to his feet and returned to the doctor who stood, head bent forward, engrossed in thought.

"I must see Miriam," he announced suddenly.

The doctor evinced no surprise.

"To try would endanger you both," he said, with finality. "You must not even mention her name where it might be overheard."

"I'm not afraid to tell the whole world I love her," cried Jimmy hotly.

"My warning is not for your safety, my boy; but for hers. Both of us are now under the eye of the Master, scrutinizing every chance of a leak through which might trickle, by accident or design, confidential information from the inner circle down to the Lower Level. Miriam's safety, your safety, my safety are at stake. You must not write to her. To use the radiophone would be as big a risk. For me to see her in your behalf would be equally dangerous. It is even perilous to have in your possession anything giving a clue to her identity."

Jimmy hesitated a moment, then slowly he drew from his pocket the declaration of marriage. With averted eyes, he tore it into tiny bits. A few at a time he held up on the palm of his hand for the wind to blow away.

"I must get word to her somehow," he persisted doggedly.

"It can only be through someone else."

The name of Georgette Graylor flashed into Jimmy's mind, a talented girl slightly older than Miriam. Georgette taught a class in art, which the younger girl attended in the community center including the Ninety-fourth Section.

Dr. Edgerton had conducted a course in philosophy there. It would be easy for him to give a message to Georgette by word of mouth, casually, so as to arouse no suspicion in the mind of any observer. Equally easy would it be for Georgette to repeat the message to Miriam, during a session of her class, as if she were conveying a word or two of instructive criticism.

Jimmy told this plan to the doctor.

"I recall the young lady," the latter replied. "A vivid personality, capable, ambitious, magnetic; but not, I should suppose, a devotee of chastity."

"She makes no pretense of being one," rejoined Jimmy.

"And she is a friend of Miriam's?"

"I did not say 'friend,' " corrected Jimmy. "I said they knew each other."

"Probably she will hold her tongue, if I can make her understand her own danger in acting as go-between. The message must be brief and guarded."

Jimmy wished to pour out words of endearment, constancy, caution; but the doctor was adamant. Only by emphasizing again and again that mere attempt at communication was perilous could he make Jimmy admit the wisdom of brevity.

At last they agreed on the message the doctor should ask Georgette to deliver:

"Communication is dangerous until the position is assured. Tell no one. Have faith."

"And now," said the doctor. "I'll attend to this at once."

They walked to the stairway leading to the Upper Level, and separated. At the top Jimmy looked down. With a twinge of uneasiness, he noticed an ill-clad loafer he had seen near them on the lake front, slouching along in the direction the doctor had taken.

CHAPTER SEVEN

DEEPLY thoughtful, Jimmy sauntered northward along the west side of Michigan Drive, fashionable downtown promenade lined with exclusive shops, clubs, theaters.

He paid little attention to the passersby, younger members of the wealthiest class and the usual throng of employees going about their business duties. He was wondering what the mission was of which the Master had spoken.

His imagination conjured up a dark vista of evil stratagems. Was the Master intent on seizing the gold supply for himself? Did he aspire to become a czar, regardless of the toll in life and liberty? Had he projected this ambitious plot far into the future, and selected his successor in a new line of Caesars, determined to destroy every vestige of democracy that still remained? Did he design to accomplish this stupendous intrigue by systematic murder of all those around him in the inner circle, except chosen ones to whom he intended to bequeath an empire?

Jimmy was recalled to his physical surroundings by hearing his name pronounced with an accent of surprise.

Vivian Ransler alighted from a motor car drawn up in front of the Idlers' Club.

"How fortunate," she greeted him. "I was hoping to catch you alone."

He did not guess that she had been instantly informed of his return to the Upper Level, and had staged this meeting which seemed quite accidental.

"Come in for a cup of tea. I want to talk to you."

The flattering eagerness in her voice stimulated him like champagne. Her black eyes were bright with more than natural animation. Through her manner ran a heady current of feverish daring that stirred in him intuitions he tried to conceal from himself.

She swept him into the club and up to a large private room that glittered with excessive splendor.

The Idlers' Club, most exclusive social organization of the inner circle, limited its roll to a life membership of one thousand, five hundred men and five hundred women. Here, in privacy impenetrable except by order of the Master himself, the members and their guests pushed emotional excitement to incredible excesses beyond the border of esoteric vices.

Troupes of entertainers were always in attendance. A symphony orchestra was ready at a moment's notice to respond to the baton. Coryphées, acrobats, male and female contortionists loitered in dressing rooms ready to perform, like actors in the wings of a theater awaiting entrance cues. Spacious lounges, swimming pools, ballrooms were available for extravagant orgies that depicted brilliant episodes in every social season.

But there was no library and no restaurant.

Eating in crowds had long been taboo as gross, proletarian vulgarity. To the refined civilization of the Upper Level it seemed base expression of the herd instinct, a thing to expect of lower animals, but not of man, as disgusting as other physiological necessities that no elegance of manners could make pleasing to contemplate.

The origin of this passion for privacy was deeper than the demands of effete taste. Most leaders in the social cliques, whether men or women, were units of responsibility, or exerted influence in some sanctum of the System. They knew the need of scrupulous caution.

Danger of assassination stalked them day and night. They tried to shield themselves as best they could. Vigilance required less ingenuity in private, or with selected intimates, than in public.

Feuds among the coteries of financiers were continual. Kidnapping and murder were of common occurrence, for unless the victim in one of these crimes had seemed indispensable to the System as a whole, punishment of the perpetrators was left to his close associates, or the feeble processes of the law.

The older multimillionaires, although always accompanied by bodyguards, seldom went afoot on the boulevard level.

To attend conferences, or keep appointments in offices other than their own, they made use of the private overhead bridges that connected all the principal buildings, including the theaters and the clubs.

The room in which Jimmy found himself alone with Vivian Ransler seemed to be alive and breathing. On three sides, from the high ceiling to the floor, heavy, red-gold hangings bellied and flattened in constant motion, impelled by regulated drafts of air behind them. Outlined in crimson, nude figures of heroic size swayed and twisted in infamous postures.

On the fourth side were two golden doors; one on the right, through which they had entered from the elevator; the other on the left, of the same size and appearance. Between these a television screen held conspicuous position.

Huge vases in corners overflowed with soft yellow light, welling up with quivering changes in degree of modulated intensity. The air was pure and cool, faintly perfumed with a pungent, oriental odor. The naked figures on the undulating hangings, bending and clutching, pulsated in a silent tumult of sensuality.

"Do you like it?" asked Vivian Ransler in vibrant tones.

His eyes sought hers, and instantly he was aware that she had been studying him intently, drinking in with the gusto of a connoisseur the display of emotions his countenance betrayed.

He felt his face burn. He tried to control his expression, and became painfully self-conscious.

She seemed delighted; and watched him with shining eyes, in which the pupils were curiously distended.

"You're beautifully sensitive," she murmured, and touched his hand.

He drew it away, abashed.

With an abrupt change of manner, she broke the tension between them.

"Sit there at the table," she urged lightly. "I'll order some iced tea, Russian."

She left him, and pulled aside one of the hangings to disappear behind it.

Jimmy drew a chair to the table and sat down facing the television screen. He hoped she would sit opposite him, so that the table might be between them. And then he jeered at himself for delinquency as a gallant, or want of fortitude as a monogamist.

He rose to his feet as she returned. She had changed into a languorous negligee. He felt embarrassed when she noted the arrangement of the chairs at the table.

"Fear is a depressant," she laughed. "It spoils everything."

The golden door to the left opened, and a young girl, dressed as a page, brought tea in fat, green goblets. Vivian Ransler said a few words in a low tone, and dismissed her.

To Jimmy she remarked, quizzically, "A musical show may amuse you. On the screen the girls aren't real. You can enjoy them without being frightened."

While she was speaking, she opened a little jeweled case. Out of it she took a small white cube that looked like a diminutive lump of sugar.

"Try this in your tea," she suggested.

Jimmy, with the memory of Frederick Warrington fresh in mind, put a hand over his glass in horror.

Anger showed momentarily in her eyes, but gave way to vague comprehension.

"See," she smiled, indolently, dropping the little cube into her own glass, "it's only a pleasant brain stimulant."

She raised the glass and drank.

With a trembling hand, he did likewise.

The tea was so heavily charged with rum and spices that he took only a single swallow.

"You don't like alcohol," she diagnosed, frankly. "I'm glad of that. I hate boys who get drunk."

Into Jimmy's mind flashed a picture of the young fellow, Braxley, crumpled up in one corner of the limousine, "drunk and rather disorderly."

He moved uneasily in his chair, and tried to concentrate his attention on the television screen.

It was some twelve feet square, framed with a miniature proscenium arch and diminutive footlights, which had just blazed up. The technique of transmission picked out with exactitude only what was within the stage area of the actual theater several miles away, and precisely fitted that into the frame around the screen.

The curtain rose. Vitascopic focusing gave to the doll-sized figures the appearance of being endowed with life, and of moving in three-dimensional space.

Reduction in the size of the living actors and of the scenery intensified lighting effects and the gay coloring. At the same time it so diminished minor defects in the real performance that they became no longer visible. Competent dramatic critics contended that a vitascopic production was better art than the real performance it transmitted.

Sound reproduction was in perfect accord with the action. Dancing by choruses, and marches to stirring music by troupes of nude girls up and down broad stairways in intricate figures, attained the precision of mathematical perfection. To Jimmy it seemed that the continuity of the performance depended on geometrical symmetry in succeeding drill formations and dances, rather than on a story.

He felt Vivian Ransler's eyes constantly upon him. They searched his face in the dimmed lighting, with restless query. They hunted over his body as if they could see through his clothing, and grow familiar with every muscle, every contour of his person.

Twice she added tea to her glass, and dropped into the mixture another of the little white cubes from the jeweled case.

Jimmy feigned deep interest in the shallow, glittering performance on the screen, but his mind was a clutter of nervous apprehensions and broken impulses. What effect might the drug she was taking not have? His perturbation held him immune to her sexual allurement. Behind it he thought he perceived the impersonal unmorality of an animal.

He wondered whether Dr. Edgerton had been able to deliver the message for Miriam. His disgust at his own predicament became poignant.

The luxurious surroundings, the writhing tapestries, suggested the trappings of a cortege at the funeral of a body that had lain too long in state.

The concluding curtain of the twenty minute television performance rounded off a unified impression of wealth, glorifying the power of gold. The light in the room grew stronger.

Vivian's hungry eyes were devouring him. The drug was tearing away the last barrier restraining her wanton personality.

She began to talk to him fluently, with a fulsomeness of expression and implication that terrified him.

From time to time her red tongue licked a corner of her mouth. Her speech was thick, but lucidly connected, and defined with shocking clarity wicked phantasms that raced through her brain.

Perfectly cognizant of her surroundings, she intensified and distorted them with the supernatural cunning of drug-inflamed imagining. She wove a salacious delirium in which she sought to ensnare the healthy mind of her young companion.

Jimmy got up from his chair nervously. She rose quickly, and came close to him.

"Look at the figures on the hangings," she whispered. "Behind them are other rooms and other figures. Do you understand my meaning?"

She caught his hand, and fondled it against her breast.

Suddenly the clean-cut stroke of a bell rang out like a command.

Vivian Ransler reacted to the interruption as if from the lash of a whip; and stood motionless, while the clear note vibrated in the air.

The bell rang again. She stamped her foot in anger.

As if impelled against her will, she went to one of the doors, opened a wicket and received a folded paper.

The message it contained infuriated her. She crushed the paper in her hand.

The bell rang once more with sharp insistence.

"It's an order," she said, sullenly. "A secretary is waiting for you in the lobby."

With an effort, she threw off her annoyance of manner, and added seductively: "In a few days you will be less busy, and then we can meet without being interrupted. Don't forget."

Reluctantly she opened the door to the elevator, and allowed him to enter it alone.

On the main floor Bromwell accosted him, and led him to a car waiting in front of the club.

A wave of intense fatigue swept over Jimmy. He remembered that Miriam had called Vivian Ransler a vampire. The medieval meaning of the epithet made him shudder.

He took his seat beside the secretary like one recovering from a hypnotic trance.

"Where are we going?" he asked dully.

"To Ransler Castle," answered Bromwell, ignoring Jimmy's obvious loss of poise. "I have something of importance for you and Dr. Edgerton."

CHAPTER EIGHT

WHEN Dr. Edgerton left Jimmy at the foot of the stairway to the Upper Level, after their colloquy on the lake front, he made no effort to discover whether he was being followed. Assuming that if he were, he could not prevent it; and that the best way to avoid arousing suspicion was by appearing to have none himself, he went directly to the central office in the community center that included the Ninety-fourth Section.

Under cover of inquiring for some of his former colleagues he learned that Georgette Graylor's art class would meet in quarter of an hour.

He strolled across the quadrangle to the Academy of Art. At the entrance he met a couple of his former pupils, and lingered to chat with them while awaiting Georgette's arrival.

He saw her coming before she saw him, and slowly started up the stairway to the second floor on which her roomy studio was situated. As he had anticipated, she overtook him on the stairs.

Without preface he told her the message, impressed on her the necessity of utmost discretion in delivering it to Miriam, and pursued his way alone to the office of the dean, where he made a few perfunctory inquiries.

Georgette went directly to her studio. She guessed that the warning for Miriam came from Jimmy Manse; but she was ignorant of the adventure that had raised him and the doctor to citizenship on the Upper Level.

The mysterious ambiguity of the message thrilled her. She read into it deeper meaning than a confidence between lovers.

Why was communication dangerous? What was the position referred to?

Georgette loved intrigue. It was an art in which she found the artist's satisfaction of striving to produce desired effects.

Sometimes she amused herself by thinking that in a former age she might have been the power behind a throne, a king's mistress, perhaps, for beauty backed her bold curiosity. Modern times, she thought, cramped the play of her ambition, restricted the circle touched by the fascination of her person. But the rising tide of rebellion offered opportunity to exercise her talent of instigation.

Her mind, filled with the whisperings of revolution, leaped to a conclusion. Jimmy was engaged in some desperate enterprise that had to do with a general uprising which would involve them all.

The fifty-odd members of her class gathered and settled down to work promptly. She walked casually toward Miriam's place in the back of the room, and halted behind her. Pretending to study the sketch on which the younger girl was working, she said in the confidential whisper of a conspirator, "I have a message for you: 'Communication is dangerous until the position is assured. Tell no one. Have faith.' "

Miriam made no rejoinder.

"You know who that's from," asserted Georgette.

Miriam nodded.

"Do you know where he is?"

Discreetly Miriam shook her head.

"Who told you to give me that message?" she asked.

"A professor who used to lecture here—an elderly man."

Miriam knew that the professor must have been Dr. Edgerton, and felt a flush of resentment. It hurt her sense of delicacy that Jimmy should send an intimate communication to her in a way that destroyed its privacy. Why couldn't he come himself? Scandalous tales about Vivian Ransler flooded her mind.

She roused herself from these unhappy meditations when Georgette attracted the attention of the class to introduce Edward Bane, notable eastern artist come to address them on "Tendencies in Modern Art."

He was a man about forty, round-shouldered, badly dressed, without distinction of manner. His eyes told more fully of his character. Bright as a wild animal's they had the far-seeing gaze of a visionary.

Art he defined as interpretation of the psychology of the times in which it was produced. Mechanistic design and brilliant coloring of the present day, he said, depicted the trend of life. The work of modern painters had degenerated to the level of drawing by engineers, and color scheme by interior decorators.

In primitive animal intelligence, he told them, early effort to interpret environment had given birth to the human soul. This soul, trying to comprehend the reason for its being, had imagined gods.

During the thousands of years man required to extricate himself from the homogeneous abundance of life, budding ideals of expression in behavior gave him his strength to struggle upward. They were his own ideals, to be sure, but he personified them in gods, and they became divine laws. Succeeding generations inculcated them as morals.

And then in the nineteenth century a civilized world greeted with delight the dawn of a fatal era. A fight began to clear away barriers of religion that obstructed its advancement.

Agnosticism swelled like a mighty question mark as understanding of Darwin's theory spread. At first the masses shrank from accepting this scientific expose of man's foul origin in exchange for the pleasing myth of his fall from grace. More than one scientist cringed before it. Rudolph Virchow so feared the new hypothesis that he ignored its convincingness and declared: "We must not teach that man has descended from the ape or any other animal."

Bane looked around the studio with burning eyes.

"We have traded our birthright for a mess of pottage," he cried, fiercely. "We are trying to live on intermittent beliefs founded on propaganda, instead of on enduring faith.

"Behold the picture of Christ that artists paint today," he cried. "A brutal, muscular body like a Roman gladiator. A hard, clean-shaven face like a pugilist.

"Practical purposes, focusing in the single pursuit of gold, have supplanted ideals out of which the soul of man evolved. A mechanical civilization rushes ahead too fast to take account of morals in its eager search for means.

"The only hope of human salvation is in the artists and workers on the Lower Level who have a few ideals left. These must be fanned into a fire hot enough to consume the Upper Level, or the earth will be overrun by inhuman, regimented robots."

When he finished speaking, the students crowded round to congratulate him. Georgette introduced them.

Chatting in little groups they drifted out of the studio.

Bane accompanied Miriam down the stairs.

"If you don't mind," he said, "I'll walk home with you."

She was pleased at this attention from an artist of national reputation; but his eager talk confused her.

She knew very well that on the Upper Level love of gold represented the noblest emotion; but she had heard somewhere that this passion was at the bottom of all evil. She could not see why, if this were true, the object of adoration were not eliminated from a civilization that all her friends among the intellectuals exalted as the highest the world had ever known.

They reached the building where Miriam lived, and stood at the entrance.

She felt a strange pity for humanity, and then smiled at herself. What absurd egotism, she thought. What could any individual do?

Bane told her, briefly and rapidly, what she could do.

He left her a little frightened, a little inspired.

She went into her studio with a heart full of conflicting emotions: fear for Jimmy, resentment at his way of letting her hear from him, excitement at what Bane had told her, uncertainty.

The doorbell rang.

In the vision-scope she saw the vivacious features of Georgette, and hastened to admit her.

"So this is where you live," said Georgette looking curiously around the bare little studio; and then noticing Miriam's harassed expression, she asked, "Worrying?"

"About what?"

"Jimmy Manse, of course. That's why I dropped in."

She waited sympathetically for confidences, but got none.

"Mr. Bane walked home with me," evaded Miriam. "His talk was depressing."

"He's too drab," said Georgette shortly, "even for a fine artist."

"He didn't talk art."

"Of course not. Revolution. He always does that when he gets anybody into a corner. Rather stupid, I think."

"How do you mean?"

"Oh, all that stuff about souls degenerating. That's what he chattered about, didn't he?"

Miriam nodded.

"He tried it on me," continued Georgette, "but it didn't take, and he shied off."

"I thought you believed revolution necessary, Georgette."

"Whether it is or not, it's coming, but not to get more for peoples' souls. What they want is more for their bodies."

"Just a fight for that, you think?"

"What else is worth having a revolution about? I'm no intellectual, Miriam, and neither are you, but we know enough to understand that a soul is nothing but a memory that hoards remorse."

"That sounds dreadfully Upper Level."

"The Upper Level is the happiest place, isn't it?" Georgette laughed superciliously. "If I were up there," she went on, "I'd be satisfied; and I know it. So would most of the bitter revolutionaries; but they don't know it. Lift the best of them to the Upper Level, give him an assured place there, and he would forget in no time his hatred of the System, his sympathy for the unemployed and all his friends."

"That will never happen to Jimmy!"

The exclamation escaped Miriam's lips before she realized what she was saying.

Georgette eyed her understandingly.

"So that's where he is," said she. "I might have guessed it. He's a spy for the revolution."

"Jimmy's no spy," denied Miriam loyally. "He's there on invitation, because he did a service for the daughter of the Master."

Georgette gasped with surprise.

"Oh," cried Miriam. "I shouldn't have told you that. But I don't see how it matters. Hundreds saw what happened—a fight on the beach."

"You're a lucky girl," replied Georgette. "Now you have a chance to get up there yourself. What do you care about a revolution?"

"Don't tell anyone Jimmy's there," begged Miriam. "You know what his message was."

"Tell!" repeated Georgette. "Why should I tell? Of course I won't."

But Miriam was by no means sure. She felt more fearful after Georgette had gone, when she thought over her own indiscreet disclosure.

CHAPTER NINE

DR. EDGERTON did not remain long in the Academy of Art after speaking to Georgette; but he was careful to show no haste in taking his departure. Slowly he moved across the quadrangle.

Among the crowding students and educators he discerned an ominous anxiety. A bomb had been found in the entrance to the free lodging house that nightly sheltered more than three thousand unemployed of the community.

Civic authorities had removed the infernal machine to the municipal laboratory. No official report had been made public, but it was whispered that analysis by the department of chemistry established beyond question that the bomb contained a new explosive of diabolic destructiveness. A single grain no larger than the point of a pin, it was said, had blown off an arm of one of the analysts trying to sweep it into a test tube with a feather.

Dr. Edgerton observed among the students many workers and persons of formidable appearance. This intermingling rarely occurred except in times of extreme unrest that culminated in mob attack on the Upper Level. In the present instance, however, the scraps of conversation he overheard in the halls and on the quadrangle threatened something worse than rioting; nothing less than rebellion.

A general uprising was making headway with cumulative effectiveness. A phrase that repeatedly caught his ear, "The Chosen Clique," seemed to designate the source of instigation to revolution. Its mysteriousness exaggerated in the crowd mind the idea of powerful leadership.

Knots of students were gathered around speakers who harangued them in low tones. One warned that the water supply in densely populated districts was about to be poisoned. Another contended that excessive dissipations had affected executive minds which bore the responsibility of directing the great industries. A third asserted that the Master, stricken with an incurable disease, was dying, guarded against ambitious rivals by only a few faithful retainers.

The doctor felt relieved when he got out of the precincts of the community center. He turned eastward on Diversey Boulevard, about a mile from the western edge of the Upper Level.

Delivery of the message to Georgette, he congratulated himself, was fulfillment of the last obligation that could drag him down into this milling underworld disquietude.

At the first corner he hesitated near the stairs to the subway moving sidewalk. While he stood undecided whether to descend or walk a few blocks farther, an automobile drew up near him and a voice called out, "Hello, Doctor, going down town?"

The rear door swung open.

"Jump in," the voice invited. "We'll give you a lift."

He could not see the speaker, and stepped to the side of the car. A hand shot out, caught his arm in the grip of a wrestler and dragged him in. Before he realized what was happening the car jerked ahead with a speed that belied its old appearance.

At the next cross street it turned to the right for one block, then to the right again, and sped westward away from the center of the city.

Pulled into the back seat between two male bravos, Dr. Edgerton felt himself held firmly by an arm on each side.

"What does this mean?" he demanded with a brave show of indignation.

He got no answer; but he thought he understood. Undoubtedly he had been followed. Now he was being taken before the Master to account for communicating with Georgette, and everyone else he had spoken to in a community center boiling with disloyalty.

Regret at having perhaps destroyed his chance of a secure position on the Upper Level distressed him. A foolish act of good nature to aid a boy-and-girl love affair had probably lost him his golden opportunity.

As the car swept on in silence more serious apprehension assailed his mind.

Would the Master believe his explanation, and merely relegate him to the status of a servant? Or would he suspect a traitorous attempt to establish a line of communication for inimical interests?

The truth seemed pitifully unconvincing. A man of mature judgment, informed that sedition was brewing, ought to know better than deliberately to place himself where his trustworthiness could be questioned.

He glanced at his captors, first one and then the other. Each was looking intently out of the window beside him. In front the broad shoulders of the man at the wheel leaned forward.

They whirled through the factory district and approached the suburbs. Apartment buildings and small residences lined the street.

In front of a bungalow of dark blue glassite, with amply protected veranda, the car suddenly stopped.

"Get out," ordered one of the bravos. "Walk straight ahead up the path to the house, and don't do anything foolish if you value your life."

He showed Dr. Edgerton the little palm gun strapped inside his right hand.

This weapon was a favorite with criminals of every degree, because of its instant availability. Closing the fist, while allowing the short barrel to protrude between the second and third fingers, discharged it. So quiet was the explosion that the gun could be pressed against the back of a contemplated victim in the midst of a crowd, and fired without being audible to bystanders. It expelled a short needle of hardened steel that made an almost invisible wound, but carried death to a vital spot.

Dr. Edgerton straightened his shoulders, and walked with firm step to the bungalow.

The door opened quietly. A man with a mask over his face joined the doctor's two captors in conducting him to the rear of the house, and down a narrow stairway into a concrete cellar. He struck a single blow on a heavy door. It opened immediately.

"Inside," he commanded.

Dr. Edgerton obeyed promptly. The speaker followed, and closed the door behind him. The doctor heard a lock click into place. The two who had accompanied him on the ride were left outside.

The room was square with uncovered cement floor. No windows broke the rough surface of the walls. A metal table and a few metal chairs were the only furniture. At the table sat two men, masked like the one who had brought him in and who now, motioning him to a seat, announced laconically, "Here he is."

"We'll waste no time," replied one of the pair at the table, who appeared to be the leader. With an odd jerk of his head he looked at the prisoner with evil eyes. "Dr. Edgerton, your only chance is in answering questions fully and quickly. We know you're a spy for the Master."

Amazement overwhelmed the doctor. He had not then, been seized by order of the Master, but kidnapped by agents of the revolution.

Determinedly he held his tongue.

The spokesman of the masked trio continued, "Your interference prevented the kidnapping of Vivian Ransler. That might have forced the Master to terms, without the bloodshed that now will cost thousands of lives."

The speaker pointed a finger of accusation, and again his head jerked as if from some nervous affliction.

"You, a resident of the Lower Level," he cried, "are a traitor to your class, to what ought to be your principles, to your despoiled country. But," he added with less heat, "that is immaterial now. What we want to know is, where is Frederick Warrington?"

Realization of the hopelessness of his position crushed Dr. Edgerton with despair.

"Answer," commanded his interrogator.

The doctor spoke in a voice husky with agitation.

"What is there for me to say?" he asked.

And then regaining courage he continued, "You have made a mistake. I'm no spy for the Master, or anyone else. When I helped Vivian Ransler neither I nor the boy with me knew who she was."

"Search him," cried the other.

His two companions sprang to the doctor, and rapidly went through his pockets. Their harvest was a scanty handful of odds and ends, but among these was something one of the searchers seized upon and flung down on the table before the leader.

"Look at that!" he ejaculated, triumphantly.

It was the tax-card allowing access to the Upper Level, and indicating that Dr. Edgerton was registered as a citizen with full rights.

The spokesman picked it up and put it in his pocket.

"Proof he's lying," he said grimly, and raised his eyes to the doctor.

"We know you were in conference with the Master this afternoon. While you were there Frederick Warrington was called in to answer charges someone made against him. He never came out. What happened to him?"

Drops of perspiration burst out on the doctor's forehead. He felt himself in a trap sprung by circumstance.

"What happened to Frederick Warrington?" repeated the inquisitor. "You know; and we intend to find out."

"I know nothing about the man," denied the doctor, "beyond the common knowledge that he was a partner in the biggest banking house on the Upper Level."

"Why do you say, 'was a partner'?"

"You just told me you don't know what has become of him," answered the doctor, but his face grew paler.

"Make him talk," ordered the spokesman.

The two others lifted Dr. Edgerton's arms over the back of the chair in which he sat, and bound them. From the sides of the seat they drew up ends of straps and buckled them tightly across his thighs.

While one pulled off the doctor's shoes and hose, the other brought forward an electrical appliance that looked like a hairbrush. From the handle ran a cord to a connection in the wall. He turned on the current.

The doctor stared with horrified eyes. Innumerable points on one side of the implement began to glow with heat.

"A foot massage will help his memory," said the leader, coldly.

The man with the appliance dropped on one knee and caught hold of the doctor's right ankle to press the red-hot points against the sole of the foot.

The position in which the doctor's legs were strapped held them incapable of motion above the knee. The most he could do to avoid the terrible heat was struggle to get his foot away from it by moving his lower leg up and down frantically. Leeway to do this was purposely allowed with cruel intent to prolong the agony.

Suddenly the man with the appliance dropped the implement of torture, and tried to scramble to his feet. Gasping for breath he caught at his throat, and flattened limply on the floor.

"What's the matter?" cried his helper, and sought to lift him.

"Gas!" shouted the leader. "Gas!"

The warning was too late. The second of the doctor's assailants slumped down unconscious.

The leader turned to the wall behind him. A trapdoor swiftly opened. He sprang through, and the door closed after him.

Dr. Edgerton detected a sickly, sweet taste that dried the back of his mouth. As he began to lose consciousness he heard, as if at a great distance, crashing blows.

It was nearly an hour later that the doctor began to come to himself. He was lying on a cot with a draft of cool air blowing on his face. His first thought was of his tax-card.

He struggled to speak, but could only mutter that he had been robbed of the card. Quick ears caught his words.

Semiconsciously he heard a secret agent who had been ordered to shadow him from the time he left the System building telling the Master the details of the rescue from the kidnapers.

A squad of picked operatives had rushed to the bungalow from the nearest station of the Ransler Protective Corps. Overcoming the guards outside they had forced riot-gas under the door of the room in which the doctor was held captive, broken in, and dragged out the three unconscious occupants. The leader had escaped by an underground passage.

Dr. Edgerton felt a faint glow of satisfaction at not having divulged what he knew about the disappearance of Frederick Warrington. Whether he could have held out against torture he doubted.

As his mind grew clearer he heard a voice reporting to the Master. "Someone has already gained admission at the Diversey Boulevard gate on Dr. Edgerton's tax-card."

The Master made no comment, but the doctor realized that a dangerous, unknown traitor to the System, one of the "Chosen Clique," had returned to his place of power on the Upper Level.

CHAPTER TEN

DR. EDGERTON, his mind free from the hangover effect of being gassed, sat up on the edge of his cot under a window through which blew in the evening air. He wondered what had become of the two masked torturers he had seen sink into unconsciousness.

The only occupant of the room besides himself was a physician who remarked soothingly, "Good man. You're fit again. You can go to your own apartment whenever you wish."

Surprised to learn that he was in the living quarters of the Master himself on the eleventh floor of Ransler Castle, Dr.

Edgerton got to his feet unsteadily. He was glad to lean on an arm of the physician, one of the house interns, who accompanied him to the floor below.

In his own room he found Jimmy and Bromwell anxiously awaiting him. The former betrayed his uneasiness by an effusive greeting. The doctor sank into a chair, and looked inquiringly at Bromwell.

The secretary took from his pocket a sheet of paper with a few lines on it, and passed it to the doctor.

"If you will both read that," he suggested, "and sign your names to register its receipt. I'll leave you to yourselves until tomorrow."

The note carried a command from the Master that they hold themselves at the disposal of the secretary on the following day.

When Bromwell left, the doctor and Jimmy exchanged confidences in tones low enough to prevent their conversation from being recorded, if auditory devices were planted in the room. It was late when they got to bed.

In the morning they accompanied Bromwell downtown to the System office building. Ascending to the ninety fifth floor the little party entered a room with walls and ceiling of dull steel. Facing them three closed doors bore nickel-plated knobs and disks that told of combination locks. In front of each door stood an armed guard.

At a small desk, Bromwell presented a card to a clerical looking attendant, who checked it against a notation in a book before him, and pointed to the middle door.

The guard twirled the combination. The thick door swung inward, and he motioned them to pass through.

"Here's where you leave me," said Bromwell.

The door shut, enclosing the doctor and Jimmy in a brightly lighted elevator. It began to descend rapidly.

There was no indication of the floors it slid by. If there were exits the doors fitted so closely that the shaft presented the appearance of smooth continuity. They were dropping into the underground stronghold that guarded the inmost secrets of the System. They thought of Frederick Warrington. Braxley, the thousands who had disappeared from Upper Level life.

The elevator halted in its downward course. A lock clicked, and a door opened away from them at a floor far below the surface of the Lower Level. They stepped out.

The guard who received them showed the way into a spacious hall where hundreds of alert men and women were intently studying machines, or moving about busily. The hum of whirling wheels, churning pistons, sliding shafts stirred in the doctor and Jimmy the awe of mechanical power and the thrill of motion. Lathes, intricate machinery, and long tables covered with models of new inventions crowded the floor space. Steel cabinets lined the walls.

An elderly man of stately presence met them. His greeting was crisp and formal.

"I'm to give you information within prescribed limits," he announced.

The doctor and Jimmy bowed silently.

"For your own safety," he continued, "slip these smocks on to call attention to yourselves as visitors who may need a warning. Sometimes we have accidents here."

The smocks, bright crimson in color, made the wearers conspicuous in any part of the hall.

They were in the most important laboratory of the Department of Expedience, divided like all other laboratories of the System, into a constructive and destructive section.

Here went on ceaseless machinations to safeguard the waning demand for human labor against the encroachments of machinery.

"The momentum of progressive civilization," explained their guide, "driving into the future at a pace there is no stopping, makes continual discovery and invention inevitable. New aspects of the forces of nature are constantly being thrust upon the attention of science, like new landscapes upon the attention of a traveler in a strange land. Each opens up a vista of unsuspected possibilities.

"Once this was the reward of progress. Now it is the penalty. It cannot be avoided. All we can do is withhold from general knowledge thousands of new laborsaving machines that would add millions to the standing army of unemployed.

"The world is in imminent danger of being destroyed by improvements."

He recalled to the doctor and Jimmy that before the System began to hold back new discoveries the telephone corporation, greatest in the world at the time, had been obliterated almost at a blow by the radiophone.

Within twenty-four hours after announcement of the new means of intimate communication, millions of dollars worth of equipment, wires, instruments, poles—supposed to be incomparable security for the telephone company's enormous capitalization—lost all value; and employees were being discharged.

This emphasized a previous lesson that the System had ignored, when aviation and underground pneumatic tubes pushed railroads into the worthless discard of progress.

"In those days," their guide went on, "a persistent aim of science in developing industrial arts was attainment of a higher degree of efficiency and permanence. Machines that would endure seemed desirable; motors that would not wear out, metals that would resist deterioration; rustless iron and steel."

He opened a cabinet close at hand, and took out a sheet of metal thinner than tissue paper.

"Look at this," he directed. "Steel of the finest temper, such as was never approached at Damascus. A razor blade made of it will last a hundred years without losing its edge. But we dare not make the formula known."

Again he reached into the cabinet and brought forth a small pane of glass.

He bent it, folded it, twisted it, and then pulled it out flat again. It was as clear as ever. Not a crack or crease marred its beautiful transparency.

"Malleable glass," he announced. "To publish the secret of its manufacture would ruin the present glass industry, and throw thousands out of work."

He showed them copper, hard as adamant, indurated by a rediscovered process that had been a lost art for centuries; solidified mercury; synthetic gems as real as crown jewels; pieces of wood made rot-proof and tough as iron by chemical immersion; paints so resistant to wind and water that heavy paper coated with them became as durable as sheet metal.

"Were these discoveries made available for mass production of countless necessities and luxuries," he told them, "the output of factories would dwindle to profitless volume. Articles of every day utility that now must be replaced at short intervals, would last interminably. Demand for human labor would fade toward nil."

"But these secrets must become known some day," insisted the doctor.

"Perhaps never," replied the other. "Modern scientific investigation twists toward a new objective in the manufacture of thousands of things the masses must purchase."

The doctor and Jimmy looked puzzled.

Their guide led them to another section of the hall and opened a cabinet.

"Examine this," he invited, holding out a thin sheet of metal that looked like the sheet of steel he had already showed them.

The doctor took it in his hand.

"That," continued their tutor, "is what modern razor blades are made of its chemical stability is so low that it begins to deteriorate after it has been exposed to the air for twenty-four hours. Blades made of it quickly lose their edge, and cannot be resharpened. With utmost care they will not last a week."

"A means of increasing consumption," the doctor admitted.

"But not good enough," rejoined their mentor. "We are now concentrating on a new metal that will begin to deteriorate rapidly from the instant of its production. It will aid manufacturers of all kinds of tools. An axe, a hatchet, a saw made of it will become dull and useless within a few days and have to be replaced with a new one."

He showed them how the same idea was applied in the production of furniture. Glass, beautifully colored to imitate the rarest woods, was employed. Manufactured on the principle of the Prince Rupert drop, this glass was so brittle that the breaking off of a small piece from a chair or a table instantly reduced the entire article to powder.

To incorporate a similar degree of impermanence in most materials used in mass production was now the aim of tireless research. It was hoped to produce a motor car in which deterioration of unimportant parts could be so perfectly regulated that one of them would wear out every twenty-four hours and require replacement. If this goal was attained, immediate expansion of the automotive industry would give employment to thousands of additional workers. Profits of the motor corporations would multiply.

"In all this," he added, "you perceive that it is the System alone that holds society together. Did it lose control of industry and finance, the economic structure, which makes civilized life possible, would collapse like a house of cards."

He led them back to the elevator.

"You are now to descend," he said in conclusion, "into a realm where research is carried on in the borderland of chemistry."

On a floor many stories deeper in the underground citadel, the doctor and Jimmy submitted themselves to a new guide of grave and forbidding mien, the Director of Occult Investigation.

They passed through numerous small laboratories in which middle-aged and elderly investigators worked in profound silence with a concentration nothing seemed able to disturb. Their faces were pale, cold, emotionless.

The slightest movement they made, whether quick or painfully slow, expressed a precision almost mechanical. Marvelous flexibility characterized their fingers. Delicate measurements, treacherous pouring of boiling liquids into test tubes, segregation of infinitesimal particles from powdered masses were accomplished without so much as a tremor.

In one of the corridors the guide enlightened the doctor and Jimmy concerning these workers.

"Some of the greatest minds of the System," he said. "These men have dedicated their lives to the noblest refinement of the fundamental aim of science, exhausting quest for traces of truth amid superstitions and esoteric mysteries in the erudite rubbish of antiquity."

This form of research, he told them, grew out of scientific experience in many an old industry. Waste material that had seemed nothing but refuse, later investigation discovered to be valuable raw product for new manufactures. Analogously it seemed probable that ancient mental output thrown aside as worthless, might actually contain valuable ideas.

By force of imagination the searchers into medieval learning assumed the attitude of alchemists and dug into alchemy with patient sympathy. To old beliefs and old forms of reasoning thus acquired, they applied the penetrating ratiocination of modern brains, seeking specks of truth that might have lain overlooked for centuries, like nuggets of gold in an abandoned mine.

"These great men," continued their guide, "live in almost Trappist seclusion. Never do they leave these underground retreats. Seldom do they speak. They know the history of Albertus Magnus and his pupil, gluttonous Thomas Aquinas, who made and endowed with speech a bronze statue, and then smashed it to pieces because of its ceaseless chatter.

"They know, too, the history of marvelous Raymond Lulli who visited England at the invitation of Edward II; who tells in his Testamentum that he transmuted fifty thousand pounds weight of quick silver, iron, lead and pewter into gold. They have substantiated the fact that he did take up his residence in the Tower of London, and did superintend the coinage of six million pounds of 'nobles of Raymond,' or 'rose nobles.'

"They ransack the records of alchemy from Abou Moussah Djafar, called Al Sofi, 'The Wise,' to Joseph Balsamo, who called himself Cagliostro. They penetrate the meaning of occult formulas, laboriously repeat ancient experiments."

"But what do they accomplish?" asked the doctor with some impatience.

The Director of Occult Investigation looked at him with stern scrutiny.

"Many inviolable secrets are hidden here," he said impressively. "For decades the mysterious labors you have glimpsed have gone on without intermission. Into some of these laboratories even I am not permitted to enter. In one of them the Master himself at times carries on the most secret investigations.

"All that has been accomplished is known to the inmost mind of the System alone. But I am allowed to tell you that application of modern science to the ancient lore gathered within these walls points to the possibility of carrying analysis to a chemical absolute, to a single element that is the foundation of the universe."

"That has been a supposition in the universities for many years," remarked the doctor carelessly.

"Yes," returned the director quickly, "but only a supposition. Here it is more than that. Gold itself may be subject to disintegration."

"What?" cried the doctor.

"Six thousand years ago," replied the Director of Occult Investigation, "gold was disintegrated when Moses destroyed the Golden Calf. The thirty-second chapter of Exodus reports this process in the vague language of the ignorant layman thus. 'And he took the calf which they had made, and burnt it in the fire, and ground it to powder, and strawed it upon the water, and made the Children of Israel drink of it.' I am allowed to tell you no more."

CHAPTER ELEVEN

THEIR first descent into the fastnesses of the System office building began for Dr. Edgerton and Jimmy a period of intensive instruction. Every day Bromwell took them in charge and enlarged their circle of contact. Numerous persons of authority gave them accurate information within limits fixed by order of the Master.

They visited the teeming airport on the Lower Level far beyond the western edge of the upper plain. Passenger, mail and express ships were continually arriving and departing in aerial service that maintained routes connecting all the large cities of the world.

Net-ray protection of the air safeguarded centers of population against bombing in time of war. The mere pressing of a button in a private office of the Bureau of Aerial Defense spread a mesh of iota rays around the city from the surface of the earth to the stratosphere. A ship attempting to penetrate this invisible screen instantly destroyed itself. If it carried bombs, these exploded before there was time for the invader to crash to the ground.

This defense required enormous volumes of electric power. The millions of additional kilowatts needed for a single municipality could never have been provided under the old methods of electrical generation. A new source of energy had to be tapped.

The first great project to transform the limitless power in the rise and fall of ocean tides into electrical energy had been achieved at Eastport, Maine, the most eastern point of the United States. There the configuration of the coast line made the building of a mighty power station a comparatively simple feat of engineering. The tide rose and fell more than twenty-five feet.

The construction of three dams maintained a constant head of water, averaging eleven feet in height the year round. At the time the station was completed this was sufficient power to generate electrical energy enough for the whole country. Diminution in leakage of current by modern means of distribution, even to points as far west as cities in the Mississippi Valley, made the waste negligible.

Heavy fortifications at Eastport and protective corps at important sub-centers for redistribution of current, guarded against danger that the supply could be cut off during a revolution or a foreign invasion.

Other sources of water power were developed in mountainous regions of the East, the West, and the South. Completely equipped stations in condition for instant operation were established in geographically strategic locations, in case of emergency. Construction of additional stations proceeded without intermission in the effort to ease the pressure of unemployment which grew worse daily.

For Dr. Edgerton and Jimmy the days flitted by like hurrying shadows. More and more keenly they sensed the intensity of the struggle going on beneath the lid of brilliant, arrogant, Upper Level society.

Now and then they heard of a riot at some entrance to the upper plain; but these disturbances were easily suppressed with little loss of life. Mob machine guns and riot-gas quelled the crowd before it accomplished anything. Ill-organized as these outbreaks were, however, they grew more frequent with the spreading unrest on the Lower Level under the revolutionary leadership of the Chosen Clique.

On the Upper Level the struggle for supremacy in the stock market became bitter. Furious selling of shares went on day after day. Vigorous buying, directed by the Master, supported prices with difficulty. Demand on the Central Bank for gold increased. Drafts for shipments abroad, and to eastern cities, swelled in volume. The beginning of a new fear spread among the lower orders of Upper Level society—fear of the future.

Channels for secret communication between the Upper and the Lower Levels patently became more numerous and better protected. The daily list of "disappearances" grew longer. That many names were withheld from publication, the doctor and Jimmy had good reason to suspect.

The ruling class—financiers, industrialists, millionaires of the inner circle—ostentatiously denied that selling stocks and demanding payment in gold could dangerously decrease the gold supply within control of the System. Nevertheless, the hoarding of gold became persistent.

Big incoming shipments of this precious metal arrived daily at the Central Bank. These were said to come from rich mines owned by the System in the Northwest.

Disturbing rumors, accepted as facts by the public, accompanied fluctuations in the stock market.

Factories that processed foods, or manufactured other necessities, enlarged production. Increased employment somewhat alleviated discontent among workers on the Lower Level.

Transportation of outgoing freight swelled in volume. Traffic in the underground tubes attained unprecedented proportions. The tonnage shipped daily set new high records. Most of it was consigned to the Southwest and the Northwest.

But the prodigious outflow of goods could not keep pace with increasing production. Surpluses began to fill the huge storage depots to capacity.

The doctor and Jimmy perceived that hectic industrial activity was bringing on a new period of overproduction worse than any the country had experienced in the past.

"I can't understand it," puzzled the younger man.

"It seems like desperation," replied the doctor, thoughtfully. "The System is fearful that revolution may be successful. It's trying to quiet the workers by providing more employment, regardless of the mounting surpluses, until the back of sedition is broken."

They were standing together at a window in a private office of the Central Bank, looking out at the unloading of a shipment of gold from an armored motor truck. Bromwell had left them to wait for an official of the institution.

Outside a cordon of guards held back a crowd of bystanders watching the removal of the heavy ingots, each in a wooden box, from the truck to an elevator platform in the sidewalk, which would lower them to the vaults.

Three men transporting one of the boxes clumsily dropped their burden. The box split open on the sidewalk and exposed to the onlookers not an ingot of yellow gold, but a pig of black lead.

Amazement flashed in the faces of the crowd and the guards. A buzz of astonishment reached the ears of the doctor and Jimmy, who foresaw that within an hour the whole city would hear that supposed consignments of gold received by the Central Bank were not gold at all.

"Extremely unfortunate," said a voice behind them.

They turned round. The speaker, who had entered the office without their hearing him, introduced himself as Franklyn Ebets, one of the vice presidents.

"We had word," he said lamely, "that an attempt would be made to seize the shipment of gold due today, so lead was substituted."

But neither his manner, nor the astonishment his features betrayed, carried conviction.

With a casualness that seemed overdone, he led them away from the window to inspect the bank.

Hundreds of employees were active in various departments. The atmosphere was alive with muffled clicking of batteries of accounting and bookkeeping devices, as if an enormous, well-oiled mechanical contrivance were running at top speed.

Broad counters enclosed squares of floor space on which dozens of desks bore the names and departmental numbers of busy assistant managers and clerks. Lines of cashier cages protected tellers and stacks of bundled paper money, sorted into various denominations and amounts by machines, and piled up like bricks. Mr. Ebets led the doctor and Jimmy from one section to another. He kept up ceaseless commentary on careful precision of modern banking methods, the interdependent checking of one machine against another to make human error impossible.

"The ancient history of banking," he admitted, "is a sorry record of miserable judgment and dishonesty. Nothing, of course, in the practice of banking can give to those who engage in it integrity; quite the contrary, as experience has showed. But application of machinery, and systematizing banking on actuarial principles, has eliminated most of the necessity for judgment, and made dishonesty more difficult."

He smiled superiorly.

"No ordinary banking operation," he boasted, "can arise today in this great institution that cannot be referred to statistical tables concerning hundreds of similar operations in the past. If it does not conform with the statistical percentage of success arbitrarily required by our conservative management, it is not engaged in."

"What about extraordinary operations?" asked the doctor.

"They come up less frequently than in the old days. When they do, they are immediately passed up to the Master for decision."

He quoted endless figures concerning the gold supply, volume of money in circulation, reserves, loans, that overwhelmed the understanding.

"What a marvelous memory," Jimmy murmured to the doctor with awe.

"If it is accurate," whispered the doctor, cynically.

The bank occupied the entire main floor, a block in area; and when the doctor and Jimmy completed their slow tour of inspection they were tired out with listening to interminable praise of banking technique from their indefatigable guide.

He smiled at them pleasantly.

"It's my privilege," he said, "to take you back to your quarters in my car."

When they reached Ransler Castle he alighted with them, remarking. "I'll go in with you for a few moments before I return to the bank. There may be inquiries you care to make."

It seemed to Dr. Edgerton that this was forcing attention on them, but he made no comment.

In spite of Ebets' evident authority in the System, the doctor felt an inexplicable distrust. Something in the man's manner was vaguely familiar. The odd way in which he nervously jerked his head from time to time as he talked, suggested to the doctor some sinister connection that he could not recall.

In the hall the doorman informed Dr. Edgerton and Jimmy that Miss Ransler had left word for them to stop in her reception room, where Bromwell was waiting to give them important credentials from the Master.

Ebets, overhearing this message, intimated that he would wait for them in the spacious hall.

A disagreeable uneasiness assailed Jimmy, as he and the doctor followed the page through a long passage and up a short stairway to the splendid suite where the daughter of the Master entertained her guests.

CHAPTER TWELVE

VIVIAN RANSLER received them graciously, but with suppressed excitement. Since her last meeting with Jimmy she had made a discovery that angered her. He was in love.

That was why he did not respond to her advances. This absurd constancy she was determined to break down.

A dozen guests were chatting and laughing over cocktails.

Obliteration of the family as a group had led to inbreeding among the aristocracy, and a consequent degeneration that accumulated in the women. Neurotic and arrogant, they traced their uncertain ancestry back to criminal leaders during the Revolution of Despair, but had none of the stamina of those rough forebears.

Weaklings among the men succumbed to their own unfitness. They sank into insignificance, or vanished altogether, under the pressure of vigorous upstarts, struggling for place and power. The latter had neither time nor enduring inclination for the women of the elite.

Jimmy's experience at the Idlers' Club gave him an inkling of the nature of this salon. He was well aware that no intellectual eagerness inspired it.

All the men present were members of the Ransler household, secretaries and managers who had been lifted from educational obscurity into service on the Upper Level. Handsome, athletic, young fellows, they affected mincing mannerisms and spoke with incongruous restraint. They were provided like so many puppets, for the women guests to play with.

Feminine personality dominated the talk, with daring allusions and anecdotes, in a kind of racy exhibitionism. The chatter imitated the clatter of machines. The sentences, abrupt and harsh, conveyed extravagant concepts in broken, jagged bits, with staccato rhythm.

Vivian flattered Jimmy with seductive attention. Dr. Edgerton she almost ignored after her first greeting; but he was a man not easily made negligible in any company.

"We were to receive important credentials from Bromwell here," he reminded her. "I do not see him."

"Let's hunt for him," she returned, lightly; and took them into the ballroom where shafts of rosy radiance, reflected from the ceiling, made a soft, dim light. Dance music, pulsating with the thump of tom-toms, came to their ears, although no orchestra was to be seen. A single couple writhed across the floor.

Vivian looked around at numerous dark nooks—retreats for flagrant love-making. Her gaze rested on one of these with the hangings pulled together. Taking Jimmy's arm she guided him over to it, and flung the hangings aside.

His eyes were unaccustomed to the dim light, but they could not mistake Bromwell and a girl in each other's arms on a broad divan in the recess. The pair scrambled to their feet in a flurry of entanglement.

The girl was Georgette Graylor.

Jimmy was dumbfounded when she ran to him, threw her arms around his neck, and tried to kiss him.

Bromwell, overwhelmed with confusion, awkwardly mumbled that he would wait in Jimmy's room, and beat a hasty retreat.

With difficulty Jimmy released himself from Georgette's clinging embrace.

"Let me explain," she whispered.

But he saw no reason why she should explain her amatory ventures to him. He took her excessive greeting to be an impulsive effort to cover her confusion at being discovered in Bromwell's arms. Annoyed at being forced into an impossible situation, he turned on his heel without a word, and strode away.

Vivian followed him toward the reception room, haughty exultation in her manner.

Georgette and Dr. Edgerton stood facing each other.

"What an ass that Jimmy is!" she exclaimed, angrily. "Vivian Ransler had you followed the day you delivered his message; but he wouldn't give me a chance to tell him that. She thought the message was meant for me."

"And you let her think so," accused the doctor, sternly.

"What else could I do? I didn't know then that she wanted Jimmy for herself. She arranged this foolishness."

The doctor drew in his breath quickly.

"I'm no heroine," she continued, "and don't pretend to be. I let her think Jimmy was in love with me because I thought that would get me up here. It did, but not in the way I expected. However, it protected Miriam; and now he's got to protect me by pretending I told the truth."

In spite of himself Dr. Edgerton felt a tingle of admiration at her audacity.

"I'll tell Jimmy," he said, and hurried into the reception room. Jimmy had already left.

Vivian Ransler was in high spirits.

"He has gone to his room," she said, "sadly disillusioned, I'm afraid."

Dr. Edgerton hastened to the elevator, and up to the tenth floor.

Jimmy was standing in the middle of his room dazed. In his right hand he held a heavy bronze vase. The base of it was splashed with blood.

"Good God!" cried the doctor. "What has happened?"

A crumpled figure, bent forward in an easy chair, furnished the answer. The back of the head was crushed in from a terrific blow.

Dr. Edgerton stared at Jimmy, stupefied.

"Why did you do it?" he breathed in horror.

"I didn't do it," denied Jimmy, terrified at the implied accusation. "I didn't even notice the body for several minutes after I came in. It's Bromwell. He's dead."

"Put down that vase where you found it," ordered the doctor sharply.

Jimmy obeyed like one in a dream.

Dr. Edgerton grabbed the young man by the arm, and pushed him into a chair.

"Pull yourself together," he commanded.

He picked up the house phone and asked for Miss Ransler. When she answered the call he spoke rapidly into the mouthpiece: "Something terrible has happened. Come up right away, and bring the chief of the house guards with you."

He hung up the receiver, and turned to Jimmy.

"Be careful of every word you say," he warned.

Jimmy, gazing at the floor in front of him, gave no sign of having heard him.

"Do you hear me?"

"I hear you," the boy answered in a dull voice, without raising his eyes.

Vivian Ransler and the chief of the house guards entered the room hurriedly. The latter glanced around swiftly, noted the body, and locked the door behind them.

Vivian ran to Jimmy's side. He was sitting with his face buried in his hands, oblivious of her presence. She leaned over his shoulder.

"There's no need for worry," she whispered. "You did what was right. I love you for it. The girl deserved death, too."

He jumped to his feet, and glared at her with abhorrence.

"I didn't do it," he shouted frantically. "I didn't do it, I tell you."

Dr. Edgerton seized him by the shoulders and shook him roughly to curb his hysteria.

Vivian gazed at the pair in wonderment. To her the murder seemed too unimportant to cause so much emotion.

The chief of the guards looked up from his examination of the body.

"It's Bromwell, all right," he said coolly. "Nothing in his pockets; but one of them is torn. Somebody searched him in a hurry. Fingerprints on the vase may tell who it was."

He hesitated for a suggestion from the daughter of the Master.

"You'd better make a report," she said carelessly. "I must return to my guests."

As she left, the doctor took Jimmy's arm.

"We'll be within call," he told the guard, and led Jimmy into the adjoining room.

"Where was Ebets when you came upstairs?" he asked the boy suddenly.

He had to repeat his query to make its purport sink into Jimmy's mind.

"I don't know," was the listless answer.

"Wasn't he in the hall where we left him to wait for us?"

"No."

"That's the clue," declared the doctor, decisively. "Ebets is the murderer. He was after the credentials Bromwell had for us."

And then he realized why it was that the nervous jerking of Ebet's head when he talked had filled him with distrust. That same idiosyncrasy had marked the leader of the band that had kidnapped him weeks before.

He told Jimmy his suspicion. The latter roused.

"It's possible," he admitted.

"It's certain!"

"Horrible…" muttered Jimmy.

"Never mind that, now," urged the doctor. "You need all the presence of mind you can muster. Under no circumstances mention Miriam. If they think you're in love with Georgette, don't deny it."

Jimmy's jaw set obstinately.

This was no time, the doctor thought, to divulge what Georgette had told him. There seemed less likelihood of a disclosure that might put both her and Miriam in peril, if Jimmy remained in ignorance of the deception.

"Do exactly what I tell you," he insisted. "I'll explain later. There's no time now. We may be arrested any minute."

He felt certain that Vivian Ransler would exact vengeance if she found out the trick that had been played upon her. No half-measures in venting her fury would satisfy her. Even Jimmy might become a victim of her rage. That seemed a more serious danger than his being suspected of murdering Bromwell.

A knock sounded, and a house secretary, accompanied by two guards, opened the door and addressed the doctor and Jimmy with grave deference. "Because this affair involves the murder of a member of the Ransler household, it has been reported to the Master. He wants to see both of you at once."

The party mounted to the roof of the castle, where three large penthouses met their eyes, and a spacious landing-table for airplanes of the helicopter type. The largest penthouse occupied a central position. The two others stood at corners on one side of the roof.

The walls of the one in the center were smooth and black, without windows. But the walls of the other two were transparent. Inside of these, scores of men and women were visible, engaged in office work, surrounded by the modern machinery of business.

As the party walked toward the central penthouse, the doctor was astonished to observe that not one of the busy clerks and managers he clearly saw in the two corner penthouses so much as looked in their direction. It was as if the inside of these structures could be seen through the walls from the outside, but the outside could not be seen through the same walls from the inside.

This, indeed, he felt sure to be the case when they entered the third penthouse. It had been impossible to see into this from the outside, but to the reversed point of view the walls were transparent.

Dr. Edgerton realized that all three penthouses were built of the same material, univision glass that could be seen through from one side only. This side faced outward in the two corner penthouses, but inward in the central penthouse which they had just entered.

They were in a big hall, at the far end of which a room was partitioned off with the same glassy material, presenting its black, opaque surface to their vision.

The doctor correctly concluded that occupants of that room had an unobstructed view of the entire roof area, including the interior of all three penthouses.

The room was the sanctum of the Master. From it he now directed the multifarious activities of the System. No longer did he dare risk assassination by going to and from his office in the System building downtown.

Nothing, the doctor thought, could more certainly reflect the tumultuous fear of rebellion sweeping over the Upper Level than this removal of the center of the System from the heart of the financial district.

The secretary sent word into the private room. An instant later the doctor and Jimmy were bidden to enter.

CHAPTER THIRTEEN

THE Master was pacing the floor, apparently in great distress of mind. On his broad desk lay piles of secret reports from all parts of the country.

A startling change had come over, him. He looked years older, and tired. Uncertainty in his manner and the slight trembling of his hands betrayed a nervous tension near the breaking point. The watchful eyes of his two deaf-and-dumb secretaries never left his restless figure.

As Dr. Edgerton had supposed, the partition shutting at this room fróm the rest of the penthouse also was transparent from the inside. He could hardly realize that the dozens of persons he was able to see in the outer hall, and the scores plainly visible inside the other two penthouses, were not able to see him. Nevertheless, he knew that all within this room was as surely concealed from outside observation as if walls of steel a foot thick enclosed it.

The sound of the door locking behind the doctor and Jimmy halted the Master in his slow tramp back and forth. For an instant he seemed to have forgotten why he had sent for them. With obvious effort he recalled the matter in hand. The questions he asked were perfunctory.

Jimmy told of going to his room, and discovering the body of Bromwell. The doctor told of finding Jimmy, with the vase in his hand, a few moments after they had separated on the main floor; and then gave his reason for suspecting Ebets of the murder.

"That man," the doctor concluded, "is one of the Chosen Clique."

The Master's bright eyes looked at him steadily.

"You're right," he agreed, "but the credentials he stole were not what he expected to find. They're of no use to him."

Those credentials, he explained, were cards checking with an index at the bureau of Private References, to be presented there only after his death or disappearance for more than twenty-four hours. Each of thousands of trusted agents had one, on which a number called for delivery of a copy of sealed instructions in cipher.

The instructions were not all the same, but all the copies of each set bore the same number that also appeared on a group of the cards. Thus a copy of each set would come into the hands of many persons unknown to one another.

Obedience to these directions after his death or disappearance, and undisturbed continuance of the system's progress toward his transcendent objective, had seemed unquestionable to the Master. But now revolt was breaking down his authority.

On the Upper Level traitors were all around him. Ebets was only one of many.

On the Lower Level a new menace grew more dangerous in the organization of corps of young girls, led by idealists, sworn to free humanity from the slavery of mechanization.

A feeling of strange sympathy, almost pity, touched Jimmy for an instant.

"Perhaps you exaggerate the danger," he said hopefully.

The Master shook his head, gloomily, and replied with conviction.

"The end is close at hand. For twenty years I have staved off mass violence and destruction, hoping to complete the preparation of a new world before it was too late. But now the forces of ruin are gathering strength with appalling swiftness."

They stared at him in amazement.

He laughed harshly, and said to Dr. Edgerton:

"You intellectuals march forward blindly. You bind your minds with false ideas, as the ancient Chinese bound the feet of their girl babies. You hamper the power nature gives you to tread the highest paths of mental attainment—to peer into the future."

"To peer into the future?" repeated the doctor.

"Yes, by developing the power of prophecy, instead of crushing it in embryo. The future is present in its seeds, exactly as the past is present in its fruits. Merely a remedial defect in the constitution of man makes what has already happened more clearly present to his mental vision than what is going to happen. To intelligent creatures the future and the past should be equally present. To super-intelligence past events obliterate themselves from the mind as fast as they take place, while the future remains as actually present as the past now is in the ordinary brain."

Great prophets, he maintained, seemed ignorant to contemporary scholars, because the latter were held captive in the present by the bondage of the past, like those eighteenth century scientists who were able to believe that phlogiston was the element of fire, but could not believe the prophecy of Mother Shipton. He quoted the prophecy:

"When pictures look alive, with movements free;
When ships like fishes swim below the sea;
When men, outstripping birds, can scour the sky;
Then half this world, deep drenched in blood, will die."

"That prophecy has not come true," objected the doctor.

"Not all of it," replied the Master, ominously. "But the whole story of phlogiston was, is, and always will be false."

Dr. Edgerton smiled at this sophistry, and murmured that nevertheless he could not believe the world was coming to an end.

"You cannot believe, perhaps," the Master said, "that death hovers over your own head, and over that of your young friend. But both of you would have been assassinated on a dozen occasions, except for my prevision and truculent protection."

The doctor and Jimmy straightened up, aghast.

"I tell you this now," he continued, bitterly, "because the weakening of my power to prevent a stampede in the orderly ranks of civilization increases your peril."

That very night, he told them, they must set out on the mission he had in mind for them.

"I shall take precautions for your safety in the meantime," he added, pressing a button.

When he saw through the univision wall of the room the two guards approaching the door, he assumed a stern and distant demeanor.

The guards entered, and stood at military attention.

"Lock these men in their apartment," he ordered in a hard voice. "Allow no one to see them, or to communicate with them—no one! They are under arrest for the murder of one of my household."

He nodded curtly when the guards produced handcuffs. Each locked himself to one of the prisoners. The quartet left the sanctum, and returned to the tenth floor.

The manacles were removed, the valet and the bath attendant dismissed, the phones disconnected, and Dr. Edgerton and Jimmy were left alone in their apartment, knowing that outside a guard stood ready to intercept any attempt at communication.

The doctor chafed under this imprisonment in the name of protection. He doubted that the fall of the Upper Level was imminent. The power of wealth expressed all around them in punctilious obedience to the Master's commands seemed too well established to be overthrown. He had little faith in the rabble on the Lower Level, even if it were instigated and directed by reckless traitors to the System higher up. Corruption of the ideals of revolutionaries seemed easy to accomplish by effective use of gold.

Jimmy did not agree with him. The younger man was sick of the perfidious, voluptuous life around him, in spite of the material comforts he enjoyed. He had been happier as a homeless student on the beach, dreaming noble dreams. He looked back upon his ambition to mount to the Upper Level as the folly of ignorance.

If the Master really were striving to preserve the human race from destroying itself, disappointment at the shortcomings of the human robots he had created might well strike him with a kind of despair. Defeat of his own purposes by mechanized human nature might sour his sympathy for humanity into raging impatience to destroy with god-like anger the System he had perfected.

And if the existing social organization was really beneficial to its members, why, asked Jimmy, was the Master so fearful they would overthrow it?

"Worn out nerves, my boy," answered the doctor. "Nothing but worn out nerves. Like many another dictator in the past, he is suffering from what he thinks is the ingratitude of his subjects. That is his reason for prophesying, 'After me the deluge.' "

The Master's pretense to a super-intelligence that could peer into the future was, the doctor declared, preposterous—a relic of religious superstitions of the long ago. As the past unfolded from the dawn of the Christian Era, the end of the world had been heralded continually.

On fear of that the disseminators of Christianity had relied to make humanity behave. Plagues, famines, volcanoes, earthquakes, wars, were all scourges, threatening extermination, that the Almighty laid on the sweating, quivering back of man to make him love his Creator and mend his ways.

The world was coming to an end in 63 A.D., he said, when Pompeii was destroyed. And again in 64 when Nero set fire to Rome to give himself a new thrill. In 70 Titus sacked Jerusalem. Roman soldiers ravaged the city with fearful brutality, burned the Temple, razed every building. The world was coming to an end then.

Vesuvius went on the rampage again in 79. The end of the world seemed just around the corner. Fearsome prodigies were reported. Showers of blood, eclipses, flaming swords in the heavens, comets.

Centuries rolled by. Rome was wrecked by the Vandals, but the world endured it. Time swept on.

In the tenth century the Huns invaded Europe. Three wet years spread famine and pestilence. Cannibalism was common. Children were lured to lonely places with promises of food, killed and eaten. Parents were devoured by their own offspring. Human flesh was sold as meat. Charters of the period began with, *Termino mundi appropinquante:* "the end of the world approaching."

Fervent Christians peered ahead with loving pessimism, and selected the exact day for the stroke of doom. Impatient Bernard of Thuringia picked Holy Friday, 922; Druthmar of Corbie, less eager, tipped March 24, 1,000, but the millennium was all that came to an end.

In 1033 a total eclipse of the sun drove human beings by thousands to strip themselves of their wealth and give it to the church. This booty founded most of the magnificent cathedrals of Europe that now, he said, filled a more useful purpose as shelters for the unemployed.

A conjunction of all the planets in the constellation of Libra in the twelfth century again packed the churches with panic-stricken human beings. Another in the sixteenth century forecast a deluge. The bottom dropped out of the real estate market in river valleys and at the seaside.

In the nineteenth century the end of the world was predicted a score of times. In the twentieth, millions believed the World War was God's roundabout way of blotting out contemptible mankind. Thousands gathered on a hill in California to be in a good place to enjoy the spectacle.

"And now," concluded the doctor, drawing a long breath, "the Master thinks the end of the world is at hand because human beings he is trying to transform into perfect robots are rising against him, and he is having difficulty in supporting the stock market."

He stood up, and stretched his arms above his head.

"By fear the Master has ruled, and called it love, like all the old gods and every human dictator since the world began. His instrument of government is turning against himself."

Hardly had he finished speaking when a slight noise drew their attention to a panel in the wall. It slid aside rapidly, and one of the deaf-and-dumb secretaries stepped into the room. He handed the doctor a written order, signed by the Master, for them to accompany the bearer.

They followed him through the panel into a secret passage in the wall and up a winding stair that seemed endless. Apparently it could be reached by many other passages, leading from remote parts of the castle. It wound upward to a small room beneath the floor of the Master's sanctum on the roof. From there they entered the sanctum itself through a trapdoor. The Master was waiting for them.

They looked out through the transparent wall to the north. On the landing-table of thick, translucent glass, brilliantly lighted from beneath, a helicopter plane stood ready to take off.

The Master gave the doctor a sealed envelope.

"An agent will meet you at your destination," he said. "Give him that."

He opened a door in the north side of the room, which was an outer wall of the penthouse, and motioned them to follow him into an arched tunnel of univision glass that led straight to the edge of the landing-table.

In silence he watched them climb aboard the airship.

The huge aluminum wheel on the sturdy mast began to whirl rapidly. The ship rose several hundred feet before the pilot carefully directed it eastward in the invisible channel, indicated on the chart by which he steered, through the mesh of net-ray protection.

Far out over the lake he turned the ship southward. It drove past the light on the lake shore that marked the southern boundary of the Upper Level. Then it swung to a southwesterly course and roared away through the night at a speed of two hundred and fifty miles an hour, carrying the doctor and Jimmy on a mission still veiled in mystery.

CHAPTER FOURTEEN

SEATED at a table in the main cabin of the airship Dr. Edgerton and Jimmy glanced around at the comfortable appointments. Besides themselves, two pilots in a forward compartment and a steward, the only person on board was the captain. He sat apart at a small desk in executive aloofness, ready to carry out his orders with incurious exactitude.

Jimmy did not even wonder what those orders were. He felt a nervous relaxation now that the stress of the day had culminated in this mysterious departure in the dead of night. Matters that had seemed important loosened their grip on his attention. The strange shipment of lead in place of gold, Vivian Ransler and her guests, the murder of Bromwell, the spread of rebellion on the Upper Level, even the Master's stupendous projects sank in his mind into insignificance.

He realized, with a sense of disloyalty, that a throng of new experiences during the last few weeks had blurred and then banished his dearest memories. Now they came crowding back upon him. He wished he had never left the Lower Level.

What was Miriam doing? Was she in danger amid the turmoil of plots and political machinations? Did she understand why he could not come to her?

As the ship rushed onward, taking him farther away from her at tremendous speed, loneliness and melancholy oppressed him.

Had he been aware of the dangerous part she was playing in revolutionary activities his anxiety would have known no bounds. She was responsible, more than anyone else, for organizing the corps of young girls that the Master had denounced as a new menace to the System. They were passionately determined to wipe out the Upper Level and all it stood for. Miriam was their inspiration.

Her unshaken devotion to long forgotten ideals, her pure courage, her confidence, animated a new code of living that was sweeping over the Lower Level throughout the land, like a spiritual awakening. It put to shame the empty reasoning of devitalized intellectuals. Their philosophy could not stand against it. Their assumed superiority, relying on courage inflated by logic, collapsed before the faith of these girls who believed they could tear out of life the ugly facts of mechanized civilization, and were dedicating themselves to this labor in the service of humanity.

They flocked to the recruiting stations. Training camps sprang into being. Every town and village resounded to the tramp of feminine feet.

Flaming idealists, like Edward Bane, marshaled the forces of propaganda.

In the background the lowest criminals applauded, plotted, and planted bombs. No eagerness to create a better world stirred their enthusiasm, but they became burning revolutionaries nevertheless. Destruction of the Upper Level would open wide opportunity for debauchery and loot.

This seething mass of sedition the Chosen Clique strove to direct. Its secret agents wormed their way into every department of the System. They corrupted the agents of the Master. Information they obtained aided the treacherous leaders of revolt on the Upper Level in their struggle to gain the gold supply, the only real purpose of the Chosen Clique. Control of the gold meant mastery of the world.

Jimmy looked attentively at Dr. Edgerton, who seemed lost in meditation, and asked the question he thought was uppermost in the doctor's mind, "Where are we going?"

The doctor straightened up in his chair.

"I have an idea," he answered, "but it's only a guess. The Master has a country estate somewhere. That's where I think he's sending us."

This estate the doctor supposed to be a kind of laboratory on a large scale, where the transcendent experiments to which the Master had referred, were carried on. What the nature of these experiments might be, the doctor did not attempt to conjecture. The range of possibilities was too wide.

He recalled the story told by the Director of Occult Investigation about Albertus Magnus and the bronze statue endowed with the power of speech, but he could not believe that the Master was undertaking to supplant human robots with actual machines.

The doctor yawned, and Jimmy followed suit. They rose to their feet, and the steward showed them aft to a double stateroom in which two beds floated in framework contrivances of springs and levers that absorbed the vibrations of the ship.

Toilet articles, linen, clothing, were supplied for them; as if a long journey lay ahead. It was only a matter of minutes before they were in bed with the lights extinguished. Muffled whirring of the motors and a sense of rapid motion lulled them into delicious drowsiness that quickly deepened into sound sleep.

When they awoke it was broad day. The ship was at rest. Through a porthole the doctor got a glimpse of their surroundings.

The plane stood in a corner of a large landing field. Nearby a building, with a travelers' waiting-room, supported a tower on which the revolving beacon of the airport shot forth its beam during the night. A clock in the tower told him it was a few minutes after seven.

They dressed and sat down to a light breakfast in the main cabin. The captain approached their table, and for the first time addressed them.

"This," he said, "is your destination. As soon as the ship recharges, it will take off."

They thanked him stiffly. The steward brought their luggage, and they disembarked.

The landing field spread out in an expanse of prairie sweeping away to the south and east, unsullied by the litter of civilization.

The magic of clean, pure air transformed the commonplace act of breathing into a conscious delight. Overhead the bright sky had unfathomable depth of blue toward which snow-touched peaks of a mountain range in the distant north seemed to point with majestic awe.

Far off to the west the rays of the morning sun brightened the gray walls of round, solid-looking buildings set like links in a semicircular chain that bent away to the westward. Between the buildings stretches of a river in the more distant background glittered in the sunshine.

Except for the ship in which they had arrived, the field was vacant. The only sign of activity was in a distant corner, where heavy trucks, drawn up in a long line, took on loads of incoming freight from a platform in front of a warehouse that undoubtedly marked the terminus of an underground tube.

A man hurried toward them from the waiting room, which was surprisingly unfrequented and devoid of bustle.

"I was notified last night that you were coming," he said; and, as he shook hands with Dr. Edgerton, added, "You have a letter for me, I think."

The doctor put his hand in his pocket, and hesitated with some embarrassment.

The stranger laughed genially.

"Suspicion is not so necessary here as where you come from; but your prudence is right enough. The envelope should be inscribed 'W. G, 426-a.' That means me. My name is William Gordon. I am Senior Commissioner of New City."

The doctor drew out the Master's letter, glanced at its superscription and handed it to the Commissioner, who tore open the envelope at once.

Jimmy felt an immediate liking for this man. Kindliness and generous feeling illumined his personality. He was neither obsequious nor arrogant; neither afraid of his surroundings, nor of himself.

He finished reading the letter, and looked up smiling.

"You have the Master's unlimited confidence," he said. "See for yourself, Dr. Edgerton," and he returned the letter.

It was a brief note directing that Dr. Edgerton and Jimmy be accorded every consideration.

Commissioner Gordon led the way to his car, and they climbed in. The chauffeur turned off the edge of the landing field into a boulevard stretching away before them toward the river in the distance.

As they drove ahead, with vacant prairie on each side, the Commissioner told them that all the land around them for miles the Master had acquired from the System immediately after he came into power. At once he began the project which ever since had received his unwearied attention.

For New City and its environs he selected a tract of six hundred and forty square miles, lying on both sides of the river that ran through the whole estate. From a point up stream above this chosen site to a point downstream below it, two wide semicircular channels were dredged to enclose the whole six hundred and forty square miles. Damming the river at the point up stream where the channels diverged, forced it to branch into them and flow around to their junction downstream, where it resumed its old Course.

This splitting of the river formed an island of the six hundred and forty mile area with running water all around it. Neither the engineers who directed this remodeling of the landscape, nor the thousands of workmen engaged in carrying it out, suspected its purpose. They supposed it was a new water power development, the construction of which was a means of alleviating unemployment.

The old bed of the river in the middle of the enclosed tract was filled in, and the level of the entire island raised so that it sloped from a flat central plateau down to the edge of the river on all sides. As this grading was done, the land was tiled to ensure perfect drainage, sewers were laid, conduits for electric cables and wires constructed, and subways built for moving sidewalks.

The rim of the island for a width of six and three quarters miles was set aside for agriculture. Inside this, on an area fifteen miles in diameter, rose the inner city. The materials and architectural design of its buildings conformed to broad, but drastic, general provisions.

From a public park in the center, four main boulevards shot out north, south, east and west straight to the river, which they crossed on bridges that could be lifted at a moment's notice to cut of physical contact with the outside world.

A mile beyond these bridges the four boulevards passed through the chain of sturdy outposts, equipped with newly discovered scientific implements of defense that employed cosmic rays and devastating gases capable of smothering attack conducted by any known mode of warfare.

The most eastern arc of these outposts it was that the doctor and Jimmy had noticed on first landing from the airship. This they were now rapidly approaching.

The chauffeur stopped the car at the broad, unobstructed passageway. Commissioner Gordon nodded to the official who stepped forward, and gave him passports for his guests. When these were returned, he handed one to the doctor and the other to Jimmy.

They crossed a cement roadway that followed the inside line of the outposts, and a mile farther on traversed a beautiful esplanade laid out with trees, shrubbery, flowers, and broad walks along the edge of the river. Then the car sped over the bridge into New City.

No lovelier prospect could meet the eye. On both sides as far as the doctor and Jimmy could see, from the river's brink into the distance ahead of them, intensively cultivated farms, painted in harvest colors, spread out in divisions of almost checkerboard regularity. Neat cottages, pretentious country residences, capacious barns, fine herds, gave to the landscape an air of smiling peace and abundant plenty.

Men in the fields waved exuberantly as the car glided by. On well kept lawns abounding in flower gardens, groups of children romped and shouted, or earnestly engaged in the serious endeavors of childhood.

They passed heavily laden trucks going to market. Invariably they received a word or two of cheerful greeting, although it was apparent that these pleasantries came from persons who not only were unacquainted with the Commissioner, but did not know who he was.

The short six and three-quarter mile drive from the river brought them to the city proper. Warehouses and shops of every description faced outward on a wide road where the trucks of farmers drew up to deliver produce and receive purchases.

Immediately inside this boundary a broad public market circled the city. As they proceeded along the boulevard they noted that all the streets they crossed were circles parallel to the public market. These contained in orderly segregation the manufacturing section, the wholesale district, the retail, general business, financial and finally the residential quarters.

The faces of the people everywhere were smiling, or at least bore an expression of contentment. Even in the financial district this was the case, a thing so surprising to Dr. Edgerton that he asked if some local holiday were being celebrated in the city.

The Commissioner laughed.

"No," he answered; "but no one here is a slave to business. That isn't profitable."

They turned into a thoroughfare in which hotels, theaters, and other places of entertainment were situated. In front of the Civic Club the car stopped. The Commissioner accompanied them to rooms reserved for their accommodation.

"You have had only a glimpse of New City, so far," he said.

"I supposed we were coming to a laboratory, or a manufacturing plant," returned the doctor.

"And your supposition is correct."

"I do not understand."

"New City is a great laboratory and manufacturing plant that turns out a better grade of human nature run on a higher power."

"I still do not understand."

The Commissioner settled back comfortably in his chair to elucidate the Master's project.

CHAPTER FIFTEEN

THE early history of the Master, the Senior Commissioner began, was somewhat obscure, as they knew. Born in one of the darkest places of the Lower Level his lot had been cast among the vilest criminals. He grew up with the worst side of human nature, torn and distorted by elemental passions, continually before him.

Imposing natural ability and practiced courage won him gangster leadership. With it came ambition for higher power; but already a rival among his associates had marked him for death.

His most trusted friend tried to assassinate him on the eve of his being raised by an influential tycoon of the System to a training camp for bravos on the Upper Level. He would have been shot down in cold blood, but for the intervention of a woman whom he had shamefully abused. Springing between him and the would-be assassin, she received the fatal bullet herself.

In that single instant the future Master was the target for both the most infamous action and the noblest of which human nature was capable. A shock of psychological readjustment waked into enduring purpose a vague dream of which he had hardly been aware.

He escaped to the Upper Level, carrying with him the little child of the woman who had given her life to save his. In three years he swiftly rose from bravo to Master. The young woman now called his daughter was the child he had brought to the Upper Level with him.

Never for a moment did he doubt that only could he rule as Master by the power that had always held human nature in subjection—the antiquated power of greed and fear. But he perceived that if man was going to endure as man, and not stiffen into an insensate machine or degenerate into a cunning beast, human nature must run on some higher power.

No sudden change was possible. The seeds of a better social organism must be planted in a new environment where natural evolution would fructify an economic culture fit for the development of human nature in accord with its highest possibilities, instead of its lowest. Science had long recognized that differences in forms of life were the consequences of struggles by different groups of the same form with different environments.

He laid out New City; but that was only the physical aspect of the stupendous project that grew in his mind. At his elbow he had the accumulated knowledge of the System, with the comment and conclusions of the best modern minds; but all this was valuable only as a collection of facts and theories.

From these, however, he developed ideas for a new political, social, economic, and financial environment with amazing originality and virility of imagination. But it was the use he made of his ideas that demonstrated his transcendent genius.

At the beginning, this labor required tremendous power in the cruelest autocracy, scientific callousness to means in striving for the end, the loftiest constructive skill, executive ability unexcelled, and time. All these he had in abundance, except the last. There lay his greatest obstacle.

If he failed to achieve his project during his own lifetime, its successful accomplishment must depend upon the persistence with which designated trustees observed his posthumous instructions to carry the transition beyond the danger of relapse.

"Think of the marvelous ingenuity and courage in this grand project," cried the Senior Commissioner with enthusiasm. "The Master based his fundamental reasoning on impersonal common sense. He drew up an epitome of it. You should know it by heart.

"First: Most individuals, from the highest to the lowest, and always human nature in mass, are supremely dominated, instigated and motivated by greed and fear.

"Second: Most individuals, from the highest to the lowest, and always human nature in mass, pretend to deny this. In consequence all forms of government, economic regulation and law rot away with hypocrisy.

"Third: Greed and fear, being primordial urges that account for the continuity of life itself, cannot be wholly eradicated from human nature. But the need for these lowest incentives to guard against the possibility of a natural extinction of mankind no longer is supreme. It has diminished in proportion to man's conquest of his physical environment by civilization; and to that extent the power of these primordial urges can be lessened and redirected by proper economic environment. Greed can be transformed into decent desire; fear into abhorrence of injustice and ignoble action.

"Fourth: A new society must establish itself amid new surroundings that will prevent development of customs and the passage of laws that sanctify material objects and make the lack of them the cause of fear.

"Fifth: No fundamental ordinance is needed beyond the dictum of Confucius—the Golden Rule which every human being above the level of a savage already knows. All supplemental laws must be conceived to safeguard the principle of this ordinance, instead of to defeat it.

"Sixth: Present civilization in the world at large exists solely as a hotbed for egregious love of gold, out of which swarm injustice, violence, suffering, arrogance and crime. To save mankind, human nature must have an environment that first of all shields it against this terrible passion."

Dr. Edgerton was eager to interpose a flood of objections, and showed it in his manner.

But the Senior Commissioner patiently held up his hand.

"Let me continue uninterrupted," he demanded. "Before I get through, some of the questions you wish to ask will have been answered."

The present population of New City, he went on, was only one hundred thousand, but there was room for more than twice that number in its present stage of development, and beyond the river on all sides space lay ready for wider growth. Sites for half a dozen similar cities in other parts of the country had already been chosen.

"You must understand, Dr. Edgerton," the Commissioner smiled, "that all our first citizens here were selected by the Master with the greatest care. Many a worthy individual disappeared from the Upper Level or the Lower Level because he seemed suitable to become a member of this new society."

The Master, he told them, in considering the problem of population began with the agricultural class. From serfdom, up through peasantry, to the independence of modern farmers, the one note this class had continually sounded in the great discord of human nature was the whine of the inferiority complex.

Again and again they had pulled failure down upon their own heads because greed led them to absurd lengths in acquiring more land than they could possibly use to advantage. They were always more eager to gamble in real estate than to improve their capacity as farmers.

They plunged into debt with a foolhardiness limited only by the too-abundant credit allowed them through the artifices of unscrupulous politicians and grasping bankers. More than a dozen years before the middle of the twentieth century, when the final forces that culminated in the Revolution of Despair were sweeping forward with a rapidity at first mistaken for a rush toward new prosperity, had not the private debts of farmers risen to twelve and one half billion dollars—a sum equal to more than one half the national public debt at the time?

Dr. Edgerton shook his head thoughtfully.

"Those obligations," continued the Senior Commissioner, "they angrily wished to repudiate, as if no fault of theirs had caused them. Through a swarm of parasitic leaders, they begged the national government for aid with a selfish fury that had little regard for the millions of unemployed who tramped the streets of cities, unfed and unsheltered, except by dole or charity.

"From time immemorial farmers had charged that they were preyed upon and cheated by every other class. Hordes of them were cheated, indeed, but only because they readily entered into spurious transactions that promised to cheat others without risk of loss to themselves.

"In no class, the Master believed, did greed run riot on the slightest provocation with less restraint. No class stood more in need of a new and wholesome economic environment."

"No one ever dared say that in the twentieth century," interrupted Dr. Edgerton.

Jimmy, who had been listening attentively, smiled.

"Perhaps," he said, "the agricultural vote was too important."

"Certainly," replied the Senior Commissioner; and he told them how the Master provided for farmers in New City.

The district allotted to agriculture, he explained—the six and three-quarter mile rim of the island, bordering the river—contained two hundred and fifty thousand acres available for farming, after ample reservation for schoolhouses and roads. This land was divided into five classes of farms.

Closest to the inner city were five thousand of a single acre each, for unmarried individuals. Every larger farm only a married couple, or a family might occupy. There were two thousand of five acres; three thousand of ten; four thousand of fifteen; and five thousand of twenty five. This made provision for five thousand unmarried farmers, and fourteen thousand with families, inside the limits of the city, and left twenty thousand acres for common pasturage.

All the land belonged to the municipality and could not be sold. The farms were leased for a term of thirty years, a generation, at a rental of only one dollar a year per acre. No one could lease more than a single farm. No leases were subject to transfer, but a clause in every one of them permitted termination by the municipality, depending on the husbandry of the tenant and the use he made of his opportunities.

At the outset the municipality equipped each farm in accordance with its size. Upkeep and improvements depended wholly upon the tenant. His management proved his capacity, and classified him as worthy of advancing to a larger holding—if he were married and his farm was less than twenty five acres—or unworthy of the one he had. Electric current, gas and water the municipality furnished at a low, fixed, monthly rate for each individual.

Regulation of agriculture, the Senior Commissioner pointed out, was primarily to cure the glaring improvidence long characteristic of farmers as a class in their careless abuse of machinery and the economic disorder of their lives. In New City every capable farmer had continuing opportunity to advance to a position of greater comfort, according to his merit.

On all the farms of a single acre only vegetables were grown. Each tenant was required to raise a few chickens. He could sell his produce at retail on his farm or to customers inside the city proper, or market it wholesale, as he saw fit. Every larger farm had to maintain a vegetable garden for its occupants, chickens, and at least one cow and one sow. The largest farms laid out a considerable part of their acreage in orchards.

The growing of wheat, which the Senior Commissioner insisted was the lazy man's crop, was rigidly restricted to five acres on each of the twenty-five acre farms. In a normal year this provided sufficient wheat for a population of two hundred thousand. Fertilization and intensive cultivation raised the average yield per acre from the miserable twelve to thirteen bushels that prevailed elsewhere throughout the country, to more than forty bushels, the average that had been maintained in Belgium for a century. Except in growing wheat, no crop restriction seemed necessary at the outset. If overproduction of a product tended to develop, the remedy of restriction could be applied promptly.

Agricultural inspectors kept accurate records, always open to public inspection, of the condition and progress of every farm. No trickery could belittle capacity; no subterfuge hide incapacity. The value of each farmer to the community was not estimated by his material possessions, but by the order, comfort and wisdom of his living.

Rise to management of a twenty-five acre farm was accomplished by proved ability to produce a superior form of living that furnished an admirable example to the community.

The exceeding smallness of the farms allowed time for beautiful cultivation, and was continual inspiration for improvement. Inability to purchase land, or to expand farming operations beyond fixed, narrow limits, removed the greatest incentive to the rapacity that caused overproduction.

The arts of agriculture concentrated on bettering quality, the only true basis the Senior Commissioner said, for estimating value in anything, including man himself; instead of on striving for mere quantity that flooded markets elsewhere with inferior products. Always there were sufficient surpluses for processing and storing.

Farmers had leisure to pursue interesting avocations.

Each engaged in generous rivalry with neighbors operating farms of the same size for rewards that no longer were mere monetary gains, but recognition of superiority. He became contented with the lot he had chosen, or selected a new one.

The Senior Commissioner rose to his feet.

"I have tried to outline the agricultural organization here," he said, "but you cannot realize its excellence until you see how it fits into the whole social organism. Let us take a look at a part of the city you have not seen."

Dr. Edgerton and Jimmy willingly acquiesced, the latter with enthusiasm, and they went down to the street.

CHAPTER SIXTEEN

THEY found the Senior Commissioner's car parked nearby in a space below the street level. In no thoroughfare, except the public market, was parking for more than five minutes permissible, a prohibition that kept the streets free and open. This regulation put but slight inconvenience on motorists, because adequate municipal parking facilities, at a reasonable charge, were available in every block.

They got into the car, and the Senior Commissioner directed the chauffeur to drive slowly to the City Hall.

Streets and sidewalks were as clean as well kept floors. No unsightly receptacles for sweepings, garbage, or papers and refuse cast aside by careless pedestrians, broke the straight, horizontal lines of perspective. Quick moving, industrious employees of the street-cleaning department let no rubbish accumulate anywhere. In every block they disposed of dirt and litter immediately, through a trap in the pavement, to be carried underground to the municipal incinerator. Dressed in trim uniforms these workers, men and women, for the most part were young, all of them were vigorous. Like the policemen and the firemen, they had to be under forty years of age.

No municipal clerical position, on the contrary, was open to anyone under forty. Nor was any person under that age eligible to elective office.

The number of officials chosen by popular ballot was not large. The principal ones were the twenty-five commissioners who performed the duties undertaken by a mayor, aldermen and departmental heads in the old-fashioned municipality. This board selected a Senior Commissioner to act as chief executive, and ten other commissioners to direct various departments.

Dr. Edgerton looked at their host with new interest.

"Then you," he said, "are the political head of New City?"

The Senior Commissioner smiled an affirmative.

"Tell me," continued the doctor, "how was it possible that among all the persons we passed on the way to the Civic Club, so few knew who you were?"

"To understand that," answered the Senior Commissioner, "you must be familiar with our elective method."

He explained that every resident was registered on a card filed in the Bureau of Civic Records. These cards did not simply gather dust there. Each kept a continuous history of the individual, man or woman, whom it concerned.

Everyone above the age of eighteen had the privilege of suffrage, and must assert it. The eligible voter who failed to cast his ballot at an election was fined, unless permission to be absent from the polls for some acceptable reason had been obtained in advance.

As all candidates for office had to be forty years of age or older, it was not difficult to learn which were the most desirable from their registration cards in the Bureau of Civic Records. The qualifications were those of character. The married or unmarried status of the candidate, the parentage, the immediate family history, got no less attention than reputation for integrity, competence, good temper and unselfishness.

If a person wishing to become a candidate had been divorced, that incident was regarded with disfavor, not because there was any objection to divorce—divorce, indeed, was considered wise and commendable under recognized circumstances—but because contracting a marriage that made even creditable divorce necessary, indicated a want of good judgment.

The list of candidates, with pertinent facts that appeared on their record cards, was published at municipal expense. Often forty or fifty persons ran for a single office, but the method of voting eliminated all cost of campaigning and prevented unscrupulous politics; for not the candidate who received the largest number of votes was elected, but the candidate who received the smallest number of votes above one hundred.

This made easy the defeat of any candidate who seemed unfit to a considerable percentage of the voters, but difficult the election of anyone by mob enthusiasm alone. The result of an election was always uncertain, but the uncertainty flickered over the best candidates and ignored the worst.

Persons in public office sought to keep out of the spotlight of publicity, instead of trying to get into it. Noisy popularity was more likely to defeat a public officer up for reelection than return him to office. The civic desirability of modesty and dignity in public life was emphasized.

"I suppose," said the doctor, "that candidates have to meet some educational requirements."

"None at all," replied the Senior Commissioner. "Examinations devised to test educational endowment have only academic value."

He proceeded to make clear the method of public education. Although academic instruction had been declared before and since the Revolution of Despair to be of high value, it had been dispensed with a wasteful prodigality. This depreciated its worth in the public mind. If academic instruction was highly valuable, it ought to be expensive.

In New City only grammar school education was free, but unwavering authority insisted upon this for every child. Young pupils early realized that acquisition of all the education gratuitously provided was important to their progress later in life.

Not to finish school put a black mark on the record of the delinquent, which could never be erased. One of the lessons the new environment assiduously taught was that remorse in any form was useless. From earliest consciousness the child learned always to look ahead, and to make development of the present insure a happy future. There was no changing the past, or its consequences, although it was never too late to begin correcting the latter.

Restricting the scope of education that was free aroused longing for education beyond that limit. To satisfy this, a municipal university provided every opportunity, but the tuition was high. In consequence most university students were mature men and women, often well along in years, instead of immature young people less sensible to the advantages of education. No honorary degrees—so often in the past only empty and undeserved encomiums—were granted.

As they drove through the residential district toward the center of the city the beautiful simplicity of the architecture charmed the doctor and Jimmy. Houses, constructed chiefly of glassite, harmonized in form and color. Evidently these homes provided every modern convenience for health and comfort, without being converted by gaudy splendor into mausoleums of dead men's gold.

All the real estate in the city proper, just as in the agricultural district, belonged to the municipality, which rented it on long leases subject to termination if the tenant became undesirable because of arrogance, misdirected energy, questionable habits, or any other reason. The municipality was the sole judge.

Nearer the center of the city the residences were more pretentious, so as to make notable the successful living and good citizenship of the occupants. But the difference between rent for the finest home and for the most modest was not at all in proportion to magnificence and location. The biggest factor setting the range of choice was the character and energy that a prospective lessee had demonstrated in the vocation he followed.

"Returns from real estate," remarked the doctor, interrogatively, "provide the city's revenue?"

"A large part of it," replied the Senior Commissioner. "But there are other important sources. One of them is the monthly lottery."

The doctor and Jimmy evinced surprise.

"Everyone recognizes that fortune has a hand in the affairs of men and women," continued the Senior Commissioner. "Science proclaims it. Of all the immutable laws of nature, the law that chance is always present is most certain. What else at the foundation of multitudinous chains of cause and effect can account for the far-reaching results of accidental combinations of electrons and protons fortuitously released to stream through space?"

He maintained that prohibiting government lotteries was sheer hypocrisy that did more harm than good. It turned natural zest for appeal to fortune toward dishonestly manipulated schemes from which all chance had been weeded out by unscrupulous promoters.

"Here," he said, "we have a municipal lottery every month. Each voter is required to purchase one ticket for himself and one for every member of his family who is not a voter. He can buy no more. The price of every ticket is the same. Half of the money received is divided into prizes, two of which are modest fortunes. The other half goes to the municipality."

Many a citizen, he told them, could point to a capital prize in the lottery as his turning point toward more successful living. Nor did the good fortune of winning stir bitterness and envy in the many who drew only blanks. No favoritism of intrigue accounted for success. The method of drawing precluded dishonesty.

To the least competent citizen, the most humble, the lottery held out month after month continuing bright promise of success that put him in this respect upon a footing of equality with the most eminent of his fellow citizens.

Every family budget reckoned the cost of the monthly lottery as its most enjoyable expenditure. No punishment for a misdemeanor was more poignant than denying for a period the privilege of thus petitioning good fortune.

As the car entered the large, beautiful park, in the center of which stood the City Hall, the Senior Commissioner called their attention to many impressive buildings. On one side the dignified halls of the university spread around a campus on which graceful trees waved their branches above benches where students loitered.

They drove by the Bureau of Civic Records, sheltering the plan of New City, which unfolded every detail of the project to regenerate humanity in a new world; the Academy of Science, protecting duplicates of all the records of research and all the secrets of the System with provisions for their slow release; the Public Library, the Hall of Justice, the Art Museum, and many other imposing municipal structures.

In front of the City Hall—a low, oblong building of Grecian suggestion—the car drew up, and they alighted.

With the pleasure of a guide showing neophytes the wonders of some mystic temple, the Senior Commissioner took them into the council chamber of the twenty-five commissioners.

"We meet here once a month," he told them. "The sessions are conducted with simplicity and dignity. No disputes in unseemly language are tolerated. If one threatens to arise, the chair has the power to declare immediate 'recess for preparation,' and does so promptly.

"The meeting adjourns for one hour, during which the belligerent debaters must prepare their contentions briefly in writing. These they submit to the chairman when the meeting reconvenes, but the documents are laid aside not to be read until the next regular session. All discussion of the question is postponed until then.

"It is an axiom of our government that public officials who cannot discuss public business with propriety, are not fit to be listened to in oral debate. The method of election, which I have already mentioned, and accurate reporting of all sessions of the council for the public, curb any tendency toward intemperate disputation."

They left the City Hall, and walked slowly through the pleasant park toward the Hall of Justice. As they sauntered along the Senior Commissioner told them that the Board of Commissioners was both a legislative and executive body.

"But," he said, "it passes few ordinances. Every one it does pass: however, it persistently enforces. The half dozen fundamental principles I told you about at the Civic Club serve as the constitution of our government.

"The directions for establishing and protecting a wholesome environment, set forth by the detailed plan in the Bureau of Civic Records, have the force of common law. Some of these are now and then embodied in ordinances to give them emphasis, but the principal legislative function of the Board of Commissioners is to simplify, combine and finally repeal existing ordinances as they become less necessary with the progress of society."

In the Hall of Justice there was little of the crowding and bustle in the corridors, so usual in the vicinity of courts. The reason was the small number of lawsuits. To keep the calendar clear only a few judges were required. When a suit was begun it had to be tried immediately. Long or repeated continuances, because counsel was unprepared, were refused.

Nor was time wasted in the selection of jurors. Every jury was chosen by lot from the board of jurors, one hundred men and one hundred women, who served for a term of two years and had no other occupation during that period. At the time they took office their competence was established for any case. Intelligence and understanding, instead of being considered obnoxious in jury service, were regarded as desirable.

Counsel for each side was permitted to ask each juror only three questions. No objection to any juror was allowed, but the court would grant in three instances for each side the request that a specified juror be supplanted by a new one chosen by lot.

Inability of citizens to own real estate, and the nature of the municipal leases by which it was rented, prevented a multitude of lawsuits. The civic attitude toward debt reduced this number still further.

No debts, except those between the municipality and its citizens, were collectible by law. The only legal right a creditor had was to establish his debt in court within ninety days after it was due, or, if the amount were in dispute, to determine that by a legal hearing.

Judgments against debtors obtained in this way drew no interest and could not be enforced by law. They were merely noted in a public record kept by the municipality.

Whenever a listed debtor paid his obligation, he could have his name removed from the record either by request of the creditor, acknowledging payment, or by order of a court in which he proved that payment had been made.

Every month names added to the debtors' record, or expunged from it, were announced in a printed list, copies of which were available to business houses and the general public. No statute of limitations or bankruptcy proceeding could wipe out a debtor's responsibility to his creditor.

In the case of a debt supported by collateral, the creditor had to protect himself by sale of the security. If that failed to produce a sum large enough to liquidate the debt it was considered liquidated nevertheless, and the creditor had no claim against the debtor for the balance.

Concerning the law in regard to debt the Senior Commissioner was enthusiastic.

"No provision," he asserted, "has been a greater cause of probity and contentment. It prevents profligate tendencies. Persons who prove themselves unworthy of credit quickly find themselves unable to get it. The number of names on the debtors' record is surprisingly small. For a person's name to remain there is self-derogation of character that is noted on his history card, and sets up a serious obstacle to his economic advancement.

"It is a sad commentary on the sluggishness of moral progress during centuries," he added, "that a sound commercial obligation could not before be raised to the dignity of a gambling debt, euphoniously called 'a debt of honor,' because uncollectible by law."

He looked at his watch.

"Why, it's one o'clock," he exclaimed. "I must send you back to the Civic Club for luncheon. A few matters require my attention here."

While they were retracing their steps to the City Hall he told them that the judges performed all marriage ceremonies. Before a license was granted the prospective bride and groom were obliged to present certificates that they had passed satisfactorily a rigid medical examination.

No objection was raised by the municipality to a man and woman living together out of wedlock, but this relation was never recognized as marriage. The parties to it, moreover, and any children they might have, were at a disadvantage in consideration for political preferment.

"This attitude on the part of the municipality," he continued, "reflects no prudish morality, nor is it over-emphasis on eugenics. It merely indicates that human beings ought to observe as much care in their own breeding as they insist upon in domestic animals, and should regard pedigree in man as highly as in a horse or a dog."

The destruction of the family in modern civilization outside New City, he said, was unquestionably the most vicious cause of social degradation. Development of the family was one of the earliest differentiations of man from beast. In proper environment family ties were strong in holding man to exercise his privilege of living a clean, upright, successful life.

Dr. Edgerton and Jimmy climbed into the car waiting in front of the City Hall, and were driven back to the Civic Club.

CHAPTER SEVENTEEN

NOT until evening did Dr. Edgerton and Jimmy see the Senior Commissioner again. Meanwhile they remained in their rooms at the Civic Club. Jimmy was eager to walk about the city without the censorship of a guide, but the doctor thought fit to temper this enthusiasm.

"My boy," he said, "remember that we have not taken up an abode among angels. What the Senior Commissioner has told us is all very well, and appearances support a casual conclusion that a better grade of human nature is expressed in life here than on the Upper Level; but we had similar thoughts when we were first residents there. Eventually we learned from the Master's own lips that we moved in a maze of intrigue that constantly threatened us with murder. Here we shall do well to remain in safe seclusion, until we know more about this new society."

When the Senior Commissioner arrived he guessed at once that they had not been out; and smiled, knowingly.

"Too bad you refused the invitation of delightful weather," he said with expansive good humor. "But it is hard immediately to shake off in new surroundings a feeling engendered by the old. Did fear keep you indoors?"

"Prudence," snapped Dr. Edgerton.

"Call it what you will," returned the other, politely, "it is what the environment of New City alleviates."

"Are there no evil-doers here, then?" inquired the doctor, with faint sarcasm.

"Criminal impulses have not been wholly eradicated. Perhaps they never can be. But theft is almost unknown, murder is rare, and lesser crimes of violence are uncommon. Carrying a weapon is a serious offense severely punished. Even the police are armed only with gas-guns that cause nothing worse than instant unconsciousness without harmful after-effects. As for punishment of evildoers, you shall see something of that later. When you understand our financial machinery you will perceive why it is that crimes incited by greed are infrequent."

The old capitalism, he went on, was a primitive, dangerous, rusty, worn-out machine. Repeatedly since the Middle Ages it had gone to pieces and been patched together again to run on the same antiquated power of greed and fear.

Advancing civilization made succeeding smash-ups more and more disastrous, because it spread their effects over a wider and wider area, oppressing a larger and larger number of human beings. The collapse in the twentieth century that brought on the Revolution of Despair, had all but wrecked society. The catastrophe that now menaced, in spite of the Master's dictatorial control, threatened complete destruction of the outside world.

The same thing caused all these crashes—an economic environment that persistently nourished greed and fear, bitter fruits of the passion for gold. These incentives taught the cunning use of hoarding, called investment; of usury, called interest; of debt, called credit. No environment that countenanced these economic evils unrestrained could develop in human nature the capability of running on higher than bestial power.

The true meaning of wealth, the Senior Commissioner insisted with convincing vehemence, was well-being; not an accumulation of tokens of the dead past, but wholesome enjoyment of the present, made economically attainable by a buying power that was replenished as fast as it was expended in a world speeding ahead so rapidly that a material thing eagerly purchased today for permanent retention, might be cast aside tomorrow as no longer worth having.

To put an end to greedy hoarding, individual ownership was limited to possessions that did not exceed in total value half a million dollars. Every penny over this amount the owner had to spend, or give away to members of his family, friends, or the municipality. The rich man was not allowed to go on snatching and hugging to his breast without restraint, until he dropped his pile of unconscionable booty at the brink of the grave for his heirs to fight over.

As all the land belonged to the city, and could not be sold, and as leases were not subject to transfer, but always reverted to the city, the burning greed that smoldered in the acquisition of real estate, and dealings in it, was extinguished. Avarice for shares of stock, the limit on extent of ownership reasonably held in check. Bond issues of private corporations were forbidden.

Interest, being recognized as usury, was prohibited, except on debts to which the municipality was a party, either as debtor or creditor. This wrung cupidity out of banking, and prevented the lending of money from becoming the disgraceful business that, under the old capitalism, instigated incredible injustice and dishonesty.

Debts—which so frequently had overburdened the ancient economic machinery until it broke down—being uncollectible at law, except when the municipality was concerned, no longer debased and ground the poor, or represented capital for the rich.

"How is it possible to transact business at all?" interrupted Dr. Edgerton; with a good deal of impatience.

"You shall see, shortly," replied the Senior Commissioner, with perfect equanimity, "when you comprehend our money."

Money, he continued, was not the medium of exchange, but a means for accomplishing exchange—a very different thing. It must be of such nature that hoarding it would be folly.

"Money of that kind," cried the doctor, "could have no value."

"Do you think so?" returned the Senior Commissioner, pleasantly. "Then you will be deeply interested in the money we use here, for, except subsidiary pieces with which to make change, it excludes all metal coinage."

He explained this curious money at some length. It was all of the same kind, paper, issued monthly by the municipality in such quantity as was necessary to keep the budget in perfect balance. Its unique characteristic was that it depreciated one percent of its original value every thirty days.

A dollar bill issued January first automatically became worth only ninety-nine cents on February first, ninety-eight cents on March first, and so on.

This money, issued in convenient denominations, was printed in colors that made instantly recognizable the month of issue, without even looking at the date in large characters on every bill. The municipality put it into circulation by paying with it all salaries of employees, and for all purchases.

This currency was not flat money, contrary to what one might suppose. Behind it were municipal bonds and, ultimately, the influence of gold, in a monetary scheme that impressively displayed the financial ingenuity of the Master, who had devised it.

The city deposited its bonds with the Municipal Bank, and against these as security, issued the money dollar for dollar.

The Municipal Bank also held the city's supply of gold in bars. None of it was coined; but anyone could obtain a receipt, calling for any quantity up to ten thousand dollars' worth—based on the old United States gold dollar—by paying to the bank the commensurate sum in paper money.

The receipt was official certification to title in the amount of gold it specified. It drew no interest, and could be retained no longer than ninety days. It gave no power to withdraw gold from the bank, unless its holder was engaged in a business requiring gold for industrial use. At the end of ninety days the receipt had to be returned to the bank, which gave in exchange for it paper money to the amount of whatever dollar balance in gold it called for.

"Very interesting," admitted Dr. Edgerton, grudgingly. "Obviously to hoard such money would be folly. Disappearing money, I should call it. It would become worthless eventually by the mere passage of time. I fully realize this idiosyncrasy is a stimulus to spending it; and I will even agree that paper money depreciating at a regular, known, fixed rate is far superior to those inflated currencies that depreciated with incalculable degrees of change in value, and caused intolerable confusion and injustice.

"I allude," he explained, parenthetically, "to such guinea pig currencies as the assignats of the French Revolution, the marks of Germany and the rubles of Russia after the World War, and the dollars of the United States late in the period that began in 1933, precedent to the Revolution of Despair. But your money seems to leave its owner just as helpless in the end. Must he spend every dollar he gets, lest it dwindle away to nothing? Has he no place to invest it?"

The Senior Commissioner smiled broadly.

"He has the life he is living to invest in," he rejoined. "If he does that wisely he has nothing to fear from the future. To do it, some economic facility is, of course, necessary, and this is at hand in the municipal bonds of which I have spoken. These embody so grand a conception, born out of the genius of the Master, that it is comparable to the Goddess Minerva, sprung from the head of Jove."

This excessive hyperbole was so distasteful to Dr. Edgerton that he could hardly contain himself. However, he held his tongue, and merely raised his eyebrows with disdainful incredulity.

Without the least symptom of irritation the Senior Commissioner continued. The municipal bonds, he said, were quite as unique as bonds, as the paper currency was as money. All of them were of the same denomination, one thousand dollars. They paid interest at four percent in semiannual installments. Their peculiarity was that the principal depreciated two percent annually.

A bond bought in December began to depreciate on January first, and to draw interest on January second. On July first the principal automatically shrank to nine hundred and ninety dollars. On July second the semiannual interest payment of twenty dollars fell due. On the following January first, the principal shrank to nine hundred and eighty dollars, and on January second the interest of twenty dollars became payable.

Thus each bond would liquidate itself in fifty years. During that time it would continue to pay four percent on the original principal, a total return of twice the original purchase price at par.

As a bond depreciated it could always readily be sold as a form of annuity, because the interest, four percent of the original investment, became a larger and larger percentage of the amount of principal the bond represented as it depreciated.

These bonds formed a perfect investment for everyone. Sold on small payments, if the purchaser desired, they did not begin to depreciate and draw interest until fully paid for. Until then they could be cashed at any time for the full amount that had been paid.

The Municipal Bank was the only bank, but it had numerous branches throughout the city. Deposits automatically depreciated one percent on the first of every month. Most of this depreciation the bank was able to take advantage of by transferring its surplus funds at the end of every month into municipal bonds. It levied no service charge on checking accounts, although depositors naturally kept these as small as possible.

Corporations and other business entities built up reserves by purchasing shares of stock in other corporations and municipal bonds. Large sums for payrolls were always instantly obtainable by cashing municipal bonds, if necessary.

One of the worst evils of speculation in stocks was eliminated by prohibiting every corporation from buying its own stock. As it could not issue bonds, it had to depend for capital on the sale of stock alone. This regulated greedy over-expansion. Shares of stock actually represented an equity in the business and attained their true value, which no longer was subject to manipulation founded on false corporate statements that juggled funds borrowed by bond issues.

Depreciation in the value of the money and in the principal of the municipal bonds was a form of painless taxation that at the same time smothered inordinate greed. The rich man whose possessions attained the limit of half a million dollars, could invest everything in municipal bonds, if he saw fit, and make sure an income of twenty thousand dollars a year for fifty years. This income he could even increase by the purchase of more bonds as the principal of those he already owned depreciated. But it was generally considered that an unearned income of twenty thousand dollars a year was sufficient for any individual.

The old rights of inheritance were not interfered with, and there was no inheritance tax. But rich men's heirs quickly found that something besides money was required to maintain a position of eminence and respect in the social order. Money alone could not make certain even continuance of residence in that section of the city where the best citizens dwelled, and had no influence whatever in political affairs or the management of the affairs of the municipality.

The financial concern and the loyalty of society as a whole, centered upon the welfare of the city. Civic interests were of first consideration. Individual selfishness, mismanagement and inefficiency in public office were not tolerated, and easily corrected.

"All this is very fine," remarked Dr. Edgerton, without enthusiasm, "but your wonderful financial set-up precludes all commerce with the outside world."

"Not at all," contradicted the Senior Commissioner, genially, "although the outside world is still obsessed with the greed for gold."

"I shall be glad to be convinced," replied the doctor, somewhat superciliously.

"Consider the commerce between New City and the outside world as analogous to trade between nations," the Senior Commissioner suggested. "The common sense method we observe in doing business across our municipal border emphasizes the folly of the principles upon which international trade is carried on."

Every nation, he said, measured the success of its international trade by excess in value of its exports over its imports. Nevertheless, it was perfectly clear that all nations could not possibly be successful by this criterion. All of them could not continue, in international trade, to receive more money than they spent without wrecking it, which was precisely what they had already done.

This disaster, he said, was solely due to greed for gold that blinded nations to the real function of money. Money, he repeated, was not properly the medium of exchange, but a means for accomplishing exchange. Once this was understood it became apparent that the most successful commerce between two nations must be one in which the value of exports exactly equaled the value of imports.

This could hardly be attained by each nation in its trade with each other nation, but its effect could be approximated if the exports of each nation were about equal to its total imports from all other nations.

New City, by making this principle control its commerce with the outside world, had found the transfer of gold unnecessary. Outside buyers established credit for their purchases by their sales. At the end of the year these purchases and sales might not balance in value, but the difference was not large, and was paid on either side by a receipt calling for the necessary amount of gold.

This receipt was acceptable anywhere as collateral for a loan up to its face value. The loan was paid off and the receipt returned to its source, when the proper shift in the balance of trade required it.

Of course, he said, this method was possible in New City at the start only because all its outside business was done with the System, which the Master controlled and made conform to the new method. But ultimately, he predicted, this method would establish itself firmly, not only for the small outside commerce of New City, but also for the foreign trade of every nation that safeguarded itself against destruction.

"And now," he concluded, "get a good night's rest. I may not see you again for some time. Become familiar with the city at first hand. Anything you wish to buy you can obtain on credit."

"You mean to say that tradesmen who do not know us will trust us?" exclaimed Dr. Edgerton, incredulously.

"Certainly," replied the Senior Commissioner. "Merely allow the salesman a moment to find out that your names are not on the debtors' record."

CHAPTER EIGHTEEN

JIMMY greeted with enthusiasm every novel discovery in the interesting life of New City; but Dr. Edgerton was suspicious and constrained. The attitude of the people made him skeptical and distrustful. Actually they seemed to have the welfare of the municipality at heart. Furthermore, they took for granted that business in general was conducted honestly.

This apparent unsophistication in the petty treachery of human nature at first seemed to the doctor almost childish. It gave him a sense of superiority. But a feeling of inferiority followed when he gradually discerned that what he had taken rather pompously for an altruistic pose was nothing of the sort.

On the contrary, it was expression of real character molded by the economic environment into the only form that made living successful. Generosity and liberality prevailed in all walks of life, but were tempered by common sense. No careless inexactitude blurred business transactions, nor did foolish improvidence disregard the important function of money.

As the days passed Dr. Edgerton perceived that this new society did not pretend to a holier-than-thou standard of morality. The citizens conformed in their daily lives to no higher code than he was accustomed to observe in his relations with others, a code, he told himself, that people with proper self-respect everywhere followed unconsciously.

What, then, was it that gave this community its optimistic uplift, its obvious contentment and general happiness?

He was a long time puzzling over this problem. When he finally did solve it, the answer was simple beyond belief.

The moral value of the average individual was not just a mathematical mean, like the average wealth arrived at by capitalistic economists, who divided the total possessions of the rich, estimated in dollars, by the total number of population, and thus tried to demonstrate that each of millions of unemployed paupers was really quite well off.

The average moral value was no such theoretical figment far below the morality of thousands of the best citizens and far above the morality of thousands of the worst. It was an actual status of human nature existing with little variation in every citizen.

There were no irritating paragons of virtue, and no disgraceful epitomes of human debasement. Everyone observed approximately the same moral standard. He had to do so in order to cope with conditions provided by the environment that made immoral living an economic failure.

Individuals differed widely in capacity, energy, education, ability, taste, but not in their morality, which was neither ponderous nor complex. Its essence was simple integrity and reasonable observance of the Golden Rule.

In morals what was one man's meat was not another man's poison. Meat was meat, and poison was poison to all alike. Ignorance of the difference was no antidote against the effects of the poison.

Dr. Edgerton began to realize that what had surprised him in his contact with this new society was not that its members acted differently from the way in which he acted under the same circumstances, but that they acted the same, showing quite as high a sense of integrity and quite as cheerful a willingness to be helpful.

The truth dawned upon him that he had always been afraid that persons he did not know were without much sense of honor, and dangerous to trust. This was the customary attitude of the well informed man of the outside world, a treasured heritage from the savage, to whom a stranger always meant an enemy.

In this new environment, however, everyone, whether stranger or friend, was confidently accepted as a moral equal, and continued to enjoy this trust unless he destroyed it by his own misbehavior. In that case the environment quickly stripped him of economic caste, regardless of whether he was a citizen of high position or of low.

Morality did not confine itself to a narrow, Puritanical squint at sex relations, but viewed the good of society with ample, common sense philosophy, founded on considerations of humanity and economic utility.

Religious belief and opinion were individual privileges that brooked no interference from annoying proselyting. No form of religion was permitted to beg support for charities or the upkeep of its own disseminators. Religious charitable institutions were forbidden.

The theory of the municipality was that no citizen needed alms. The individual who became economically deficient because of any reason had the right to look to the municipality for aid in proportion to his merit, indicated by the record of his life.

To build up and maintain a high reputation by worthy living was of first importance to everyone. Accomplishment of this assured a secure and comfortable old age, no matter what misfortune might befall.

Religious services were conducted every Sunday in various municipal halls. They were all much alike, without any ritual of a specific creed.

Dr. Edgerton and Jimmy attended several and found them inspiring and charged, which went to reimburse the municipality for rental of the auditorium and to pay for the music and the speaker who delivered the sermon.

They perceived that the general religious belief was that the Creator of the universe was too august a power to be understood and explained by man. Every human being had a little spark of divine creative power, and could fan it into greater brightness by his own efforts. To suppose that God designated any person to teach man the mysteries of creation and the qualities of infinite mind and spirit was regarded as so absurdly egotistical in him who set himself up as such an interpreter as to deserve nothing but derision.

Nor did it seem to the citizens anything but half-witted to suppose that the Creator of universes pursuing their trackless way through space, could be palliated, pleased and influenced by the petty gimcracks of ancient religious observances. A Creator, self-endowed with omnipotence, limitless wisdom, perfect understanding, was presumed to have, at the very least, a commensurate sense of humor.

The commercial customs of the city were a source of endless interest to the two visitors. The inner municipality, laid out like a huge wheel of which the hub was the park containing the City Hall and other public buildings, was divided by the four main boulevards into four equal sectors. The dividing boulevards were the only streets that cut the rim and went on through the agricultural section and across the bridges over the river.

All the sectors provided much the same facilities for residence and business. To the doctor and Jimmy the most fascinating thoroughfare was the wide public market that circled the inner city; and the most intriguing institution situated there—in each sector—was the Municipal Bazaar.

This was for the disposal of surplus, shopworn and secondhand merchandise of every kind. The municipality, acting as agent for merchants or others wishing to dispose of anything, charged a small commission for services as salesman. It conducted the bazaar on a curious principle. The price of everything offered for sale automatically depreciated at the rate of ten percent a day. The consignor of the articles set the initial price, but had no further Control. Any article that had not been sold at the end of ten days was given away for nothing to the first person who asked for it. Anything undisposed of at the end of two weeks was destroyed.

The effect of this method was most beneficial to those of the public with small incomes and also to business. The former often got the opportunity to buy what they might not have been able to afford at regular prices. Retail merchants after conducting their own bargain sales, could always clean out remnants of old stock by turning them over to the bazaar.

To manufacturers the benefit was greatest of all. They were restrained from rushing into overproduction. They were not anxious to overstock retailers, even if the latter were foolish enough to want to take on larger lines than they could profitably handle. Obviously it was disadvantageous for any producer to have his brands of goods being sold in the bazaar at depreciating prices. That argued that his output had an insufficient market, and consequently might not be as desirable as advertised.

As surplus stocks of food were disposed of in the same way, farmers always had before them a wise, impersonal admonition against overproduction, and a practical demonstration of the persistence of demand for various products. Furthermore, the municipality was able to make its purchases of stores for hospitals and other institutions on a sound, economical basis.

No private hospitals were permitted. In each sector the municipality maintained a civic hospital where the service was graded from free to the most expensive. The cost of treatment was not based upon medical attention—all patients received the best of this—but upon the luxury of surroundings, and the privilege of choosing physicians and nurses.

The patient of moderate income was able to afford privacy and comfort compatible with his scale of living. The number of free patients was always small, for it was thought to be disgraceful to become a public beneficiary unless the circumstances of the patient forced him to exercise that right.

The fees charged by physicians, like those charged by lawyers, were reasonable. The practitioner in a learned profession was believed to be engaged in a cultural calling that provided a higher satisfaction than manual labor, whether skilled or otherwise. He was accorded a recognition of superiority which assured him ease and a competence late in life.

Relatively, the unskilled worker received higher wages than the monetary returns from any other form of economic effort. Having less intellectual value to the community, and less ability to appreciate the higher things of life, he was well paid for the hard, manual work he did. But his Willingness to remain a laborer rated his standing in the community. If he lived a worthy life he was sure of comfort in his old age, but not on so high a scale of living as a skilled artisan, a physician, a lawyer or a teacher, who might have earned less money during the same period.

On several occasions Dr. Edgerton and Jimmy drove out across the river to the beautiful esplanade that ran all round the city, providing a magnificent broad boulevard lined with trees, shrubs and flowers that formed a band of parks some ninety miles in circumference. Beyond it were athletic fields, baseball parks and football gridirons.

In driving along the esplanade the doctor and Jimmy noticed several strange, windowless buildings set in beautiful surroundings. These, they detected at once, were built of univision glass, which they had first seen as a material for building construction in the penthouses on the roof of Ransler Castle. The transparent side of the glass was turned inward, so that from the outside the buildings looked merely like models of attractive architecture in black onyx.

The chauffeur informed them that these buildings were houses for the moral readjustment of persons guilty of misdemeanors. The prisoners were confined in separate, comfortable cells. The purpose was to correct the distortion in their moral point of view, which had led to vicious acts.

Although they were not objects of the curious gaze of the public, they were able to look out at life going on all around them under its most pleasing aspect. They could see the trees and flowers, the strollers on the esplanade, the stream of motor cars with laughing occupants. No higher form of corrective punishment than this, it was thought, could be devised for wrong-doers who were not incorrigible.

But only first offenders were locked in these pleasant prisons. Here they had the opportunity to attain full realization of their folly, and reconstruct the outlook on life that had led to it. The act of which each was guilty was entered on his card of record, but this bad mark was erased at the end of five years after his release if during that time he had proved himself worthy of being restored to the full political and economic confidence, which only a clean record established.

Prisoners for more serious offenses, and those found guilty a second time of misdemeanors, were treated in a different way. They were confined in univision glass cells situated on the lower floor of the round buildings that formed the chain of outposts a mile beyond the river. In these cells, however, the univision glass was reversed, so that the prisoners at all times were under the eye of guards outside and could be observed by visitors who were allowed to look at them on certain visiting days, but not allowed to communicate with them.

This arrangement, it was believed, forced upon the prisoners themselves and upon society in general the realization that here were persons unfit to be trusted by the community. They had sunk so low beneath the moral level that must be maintained to make life secure for society as a whole, that they required the same constant vigilance as dangerous animals.

Capital punishment was prohibited, but the prisoner convicted of murder was placed in a cell which adjoined a gas chamber, entrance into which resulted in instant death.

There was only one sentence for murder, imprisonment for life. No circumstances mitigated it. Nor was there possibility of pardon or parole after conviction. The only escape from serving the full sentence was by suicide in the prison gas chamber.

When Dr. Edgerton asked the course of procedure in cases where the defense of insanity was introduced, he was astounded at the answer.

"That plea," the captain of the guard at one of the outposts told him, "is never introduced, for the simple reason that all crime is regarded as an expression of insanity in some degree. Cases of violent insanity are treated exactly like cases of murder. The sufferer is confined for life, with the opportunity to commit suicide."

Such a thing as "temporary insanity" was not recognized. A person subject to spasms of mad violence was considered permanently deranged and more dangerous than one continuously incompetent, because his intervals of seeming sanity made it possible, if he were allowed at large, to commit acts of violence against unsuspecting persons wholly unprepared to safeguard themselves.

Mental defectives of all kinds, except cases of feeblemindedness from old age, were removed from all association with society at the earliest discovery of their infirmity. As a result of this solicitude, there was little chance of inherited insanity or mental weakness.

Persons crippled physically were given every advantage in a special institution. They were educated to regard their physical defect as a handicap which, although a misfortune, was no cause for a feeling of inferiority. It provided a better opportunity than any normal person enjoyed to obtain a careful mental training at the expense of the municipality, and to attain the highest intellectual value to the community.

Suicide was looked upon as a form of mental weakness probably due to some malady. It was not forbidden by law, because no normal individual, it was thought, could be so lacking in robust mentality as to ally himself with adverse fortune to the extent of taking his own life.

Anyone contemplating suicide, whether because of ill health, family trouble, business difficulty, or any other reason, could consult in strictest confidence a member of the Municipal Advisory Board composed of five men and five women of maturity, with wide experience in living. The unfortunate met with sympathy and understanding. He was certain to receive encouragement; good homely advice and such aid as was possible that did not require providing money for the payment of debts.

If he refused, or was unable, to drive out of his mind the desire to end his life, it was concluded that he was insane. In that case the commission immediately provided means for the unfortunate to carry out his decision as comfortably and decently as possible. He was confined in a pleasant cell, with access to a gas chamber, in one of the univision buildings on the esplanade, from which he could look out, without being seen, at happy people enjoying themselves in the beautiful park all around him.

If he did not kill himself within the first day or two of his incarceration, seldom did he commit suicide at all. A week of seclusion usually affected a complete cure, and the patient was released to take up active life again with the healthy purpose of overcoming the conditions that had caused his acute hypochondria.

Dr. Edgerton, as time passed, became more impressed with the sanity and excellence of life in New City, but it aroused in him no such enthusiastic commendation as it did in Jimmy.

"Unquestionably," said the doctor, "the Master has established here a better environment for the development of humanity, but has it destroyed in human nature the love of gold?"

They were sitting in their rooms late in the October afternoon. For more than six weeks they had been studying the new society without guidance or interference. They had found it easy to make acquaintances when they wished; easy to enjoy uninterrupted privacy when that seemed desirable.

"No one here is greedy for gold," replied Jimmy.

"That I grant you," returned Dr. Edgerton, "but this community is an infinitesimal spot of humanity amid the teeming populations of the Earth. It is segregated and shielded, but the greed for gold rages outside as inordinately as ever."

This terrible greed, he told Jimmy, was the slow growth of thousands of years. Long before gold came into use as money religious worship had incited love of it.

"The earliest passion for gold," he continued, "grew out of its fancied resemblance to the sun in the primitive minds of sun worshipers. Later the alchemists called it 'sol.' "

He told the younger man how Babylonian and Assyrian temples, dedicated to the Sun God, blazed with gold. How the ancient Egyptians decorated their women with gold ornaments. How the Greeks adopted this custom. How the Lydians, descended from Lud, son of Shem, son of Noah, invented the coining of gold into money.

"And remember, my boy," he went on, "that New City is itself founded on the power of gold. Gold bought all this land, built all these handsome civic buildings. Uncoined gold in the Municipal Bank is the powerful influence behind the disappearing paper money and the depreciating municipal bonds."

He shook his head thoughtfully.

"If the Master could destroy the value of gold," he continued musingly, "this new society would be impregnable, and might well found a world in which humanity would be safe from greed. But how can he do that? Unless," he added as an afterthought, "unless the System's Department of Occult Investigation really has discovered a process to make gold disintegrate into worthless rubbish."

CHAPTER NINETEEN

JIMMY sat thinking over Dr. Edgerton's last words. Could it be possible that the Master did know a process to disintegrate gold? Was this the means on which he counted to eliminate greed from the world, before it drove a hectic civilization to ruinous culmination?

Even if he did possess this secret, had he time to make effective use of it? How much longer could he ward off the dangers of assassination that were hemming him?

A wave of fierce loyalty swept over Jimmy, and set his nerves afire with impatience to rally to the Master's protection.

His own heated thinking and Dr. Edgerton's more sober meditation were interrupted by the entrance of the Senior Commissioner. They had not seen him for a long time and greeted him heartily; but his manner was grave.

"I'm sorry to tell you," he informed them, "that you must cut your visit short. I've just been talking with the Master over the private ray-phone from my office in the City Hall to his sanctum on the roof of Ransler Castle. Revolt against the System has made resistless headway."

He declared that if the Master were assassinated, or the System overthrown even without his death, the country would flame with civil war. Nothing could prevent it.

"To shield New City in event of such a catastrophe," he continued, "the Master has been pushing the final preparations. These are now complete. I'll give you a full report in duplicate to deliver to him at the earliest moment."

That this report should fall into no intervening hands was essential. It must be conveyed to the Master, who would meet the airship in which they were to return that night, the instant it landed on the roof of Ransler Castle. Impressively the Senior Commissioner added: "Should any disaster befall before you arrive—assassination of the Master, or overthrow of the System—destroy these copies."

"Is the danger so great as that?" gasped Jimmy.

"The Master may be dead, or a prisoner, before you get there. If he isn't waiting for you, be warned. Don't allow yourselves to be deceived. He will delegate no one to meet you. If he's not on the landing-table when your ship alights on the roof of Ransler Castle, do not disembark until you've each destroyed your copy of the report."

He took the two copies from his pocket, and, scanning the subdivisions in one of them, quickly gave an epitome of the contents.

An enormous volume of stores, shipped to New City during recent weeks, had been classified, inventoried and packed away in warehouses and underground depots. The community was self-sufficient in every way, but the Master insisted on its accumulating sufficient food supply to last several years in case of unprecedented crop failures. Stocks of every useful tool and implement crowded space set aside for that purpose.

All this subsistence and merchandise was the property of the municipality, not to be distributed except in emergency, and then only as required under civic direction.

The Master doubted that these huge stores would have to be drawn upon. Ultimately they could be destroyed; but in the meantime, if the System was overthrown and war or anarchy ravaged the country. New City must remain untainted by the fear of lack of sustenance.

The defense against invasion was impregnable. Quantities of oil and gasoline were on hand. Electric power stations within the city limits stood ready to provide all the energy required if transmission of current from the hydro-station in the distant mountains were cut off.

A broad circumference, several miles beyond the encircling chain of outposts, was mined with super-explosives which, if discharged, would surround the vacant outskirts of the city with a wide band of torn and rough terrain difficult to cross. This was within range of poison gas and cosmic-ray machine guns with which the outposts were equipped to combat any form of attack.

Net-ray protection defended the air to a distance far beyond the outposts. No ship could penetrate it without being instantly wrecked.

As the Senior Commissioner checked off these facts set forth in the report, conviction grew in the minds of Dr. Edgerton and Jimmy that no matter what degree of ruin engulfed the outside world New City would be able to stand against it unharmed and secure. But pushing these gigantic preparations emphasized the imminence of the peril threatening the Master.

Dr. Edgerton, whose confidence in the enduring quality of an existing order was greater than Jimmy's, found it difficult to believe that the Upper Level was menaced by actual demolition.

"Much has happened since you left," the Senior Commissioner told him. "The Master is hedged in by enemies. No longer does he dare give orders to many of his formerly most trusted aids, lest he bring upon himself open revolt in new quarters.

The Senior Commissioner gave one copy of the report to Dr. Edgerton, and the other to Jimmy.

"Each of you," he directed, "had better suspend your copy by a cord around the neck inside your clothing."

Dr. Edgerton took off his coat and shirt to comply with this suggestion. Jimmy followed his example. The danger this device implied made him realize what they had hardly considered before—their own peril in the undertaking that confronted them. But neither felt the slightest inclination to dodge this unexpected risk. To the doctor, in spite of clear logic that proved to him the danger that lay ahead, the intimation that returning to the Master as a courier might be a life-and-death venture seemed dreamily fantastic.

They did not leave the Civic Club until long after dark. The Senior Commissioner drove them to the airport. At the deserted landing field they waited for the arrival of the airship.

The beacon on the tower revolved majestically.

"That light," remarked the Senior Commissioner, "will not be turned on again, until the Master orders it—to assist in his escape, I hope. This airport has no place on any of the aerial maps. The site of New City is marked only as a spot to be avoided because of net-ray protection. The few who know its location suppose it to be a country estate belonging to the Master."

Looking to the northeast, they saw the helicopter plane approaching. It made a perfect landing near where they stood. Dr. Edgerton and Jimmy shook hands with the Senior Commissioner and climbed aboard.

It was the ship that had brought them to New City more than six weeks before. The same steward helped them with their luggage; the same, aloof captain bowed to them stiffly when they entered the main cabin.

They sat down at the same table, but Jimmy had no feeling of relaxation. His mind was alert. Neither he nor the doctor had any thought of going to bed. They settled back in their easy chairs, and each tried to bring order out of the mob of ideas that stormed his mind.

Every minute, Jimmy mused, brought him nearer to Miriam. He longed to see her. It seemed as if they had been separated for years.

No doubt of her constancy touched him; no doubt that she would perfectly understand the wisdom of his not attempting to communicate with her, in spite of the anxiety his silence might have caused.

He was eager to tell her about New City, to explain that the Master was misunderstood, unjustly feared and hated.

The hours slipped by as the ship roared through the blackness of the night. The doctor and Jimmy were becoming drowsy, when a slackening of speed aroused them.

They pulled their chairs to a wide window on the port side and looked out. In the distance a glow of yellow light hung over the metropolis like a golden cloud. The ship drove out over the lake south of the city and turned directly north.

They gazed through the window with an intentness that made them oblivious to everything else. Was the Master awaiting their arrival, or was he already a prisoner, or the victim of some assassin?

They heard no sound behind them, and were taken wholly unawares when each was seized by two bravos, and helplessly handcuffed.

Their chairs were whirled round and they saw the cabin filled with silent men. The captain of the ship remained at his desk unmoved, looking to the leader of the kidnapping band for orders. This was Ebets, who made no attempt to conceal his identity.

His brazen attitude told more impressively than the Senior Commissioner's warning to what heights confidence in the outcome of the revolt had risen. Ebets addressed them curtly: "You have returned just in time to see the abdication of the Master. You will help accomplish it."

He smiled cruelly, and ordered two of his men to gag the doctor and Jimmy.

The ship, moving slowly, turned westward and headed from the lake into the channel through the net-ray protection to the landing-table on Ransler Castle.

The bravos dragged the chairs in which Dr. Edgerton and Jimmy still sat, away from proximity to the window. Then three of them, keeping the prisoners covered with guns, retired into inconspicuous corners.

Gently the ship landed. The steward opened the door quickly, and the captain hurried down the steps. The doctor and Jimmy heard him greet the Master.

Ebets and one young bravo, gun in hand, waited a moment to give the Master time to approach the ship. Then they climbed out of a window on the opposite side, dropped to the landing-table, and ran one around the bow and the other around the stern to come upon the Master from each side, as he stood looking up expectantly at the open doorway for the doctor and Jimmy to disembark.

The ruse was executed quickly. Only a few stern commands were audible, and the Master, at the point of two guns, entered the cabin, with Ebets, the young bravo and the captain close behind him.

The motors whirred with sudden increase of speed, and the ship rose swiftly. It made its way through the channel out over the lake again, and floated stationary high above the water invisible in the darkness below.

The bravos who had remained in the background stepped forward briskly, pulled aside the table in the center of the cabin and turned back the floor covering. On the bare spot they placed a steel chair, and began to rope the Master into it.

Not a word did he speak. With no sign of emotion he glanced around the cabin, and nodded to Dr. Edgerton and Jimmy, handcuffed and gagged.

His danger, Jimmy thought, keyed him up like a tonic. His expression betrayed no uneasiness. The hand he lifted to allow the passing of the rope around his body was without a tremor.

Ebets looked on with a satisfaction he made no effort to hide. When the Master was securely bound, the revolutionary leader motioned his helpers, the captain and the steward to withdraw. They retired into the after saloon, closing the sliding door tight behind them.

Ebets sat down with exaggerated assurance. On the table beside him lay an electric push button attached to a cord that ran to the floor. He eyed the Master arrogantly, and spoke in tones he tried to make coolly deliberate.

"George Ransler," he said, "you've come to the end of your dictatorship."

The Master made no reply.

"You alone," Ebets continued, "know a secret we must have. That secret is not yours by right of discovery. It was divulged to you years ago by a trusting visionary Edward Manse—whose son, gagged and manacled before your eyes, you also tricked into your service. The reward the father got for telling his discovery was imprisonment and finally death."

Jimmy stared with horrified amazement. Could it be true the Master was guilty of this treachery? Intuition told him that it was true. Tears of disappointment and anger blinded him.

"You've kept the secret well," he heard Ebets continue, "but the nature of it is known. You have instigated the supposition that it concerns a process by which gold can be disintegrated into worthless rubbish; but that is not its nature. Your secret is not a process to disintegrate gold, but a process to manufacture gold."

The speaker sprang to his feet, his eyes blazing with exultation. He shook his finger vehemently, and his head jerked grotesquely with nervous tension.

"That secret," he cried with furious determination, "you must disclose to me, here and now. Then you will be returned to the Upper Level in safety to continue as Master under the orders of the Chosen Clique. I give you one minute to agree." He laid his watch on the table.

"If you refuse," he added softly, "I shall press this button before me. The trap door under your chair will fall away beneath you, and you will plunge to death."

CHAPTER TWENTY

THE Master looked at the leader of the Chosen Clique with contemptuous indifference. "One minute is not enough for you to make an important decision."

"The decision is not for me to make," sneered Ebets. "Listen to me," rejoined the Master sternly. "I've manufactured tons of gold. The process is so simple that anyone can employ it; the cost of manufacture is almost nothing. Efforts of traitors to the System, like yourself, to acquire the gold supply are futile. It has no limit."

"I want the secret!" cried the other, impatiently. "What is the secret? You're not fool enough to lose your life rather than tell it. Agree to write out the formula for me, and I'll release you at once."

The Master smiled with calm superiority.

"If that secret suddenly became known, the economic structure would collapse like a burst balloon."

"But it will not become known," protested Ebets.

His eyes glittered, and folds of greed about his mouth tightened into deeper creases.

The Master laughed cynically.

"You'd be more anxious than ever to get me out of the way. With power to marshal unlimited quantities of gold, you'd try to rule the world."

Ebets face flamed with anger.

"Keep the secret, and be damned," he cried. "You can't prevent the Chosen Clique from seizing the billions of gold that stand to the credit of the System."

He reached toward the table.

"Don't press that button," admonished the Master sharply, "or gold will be worth less than the wooden blocks that children play with."

Ebets' hand jerked back as if it had touched red-hot iron.

The Master's hard voice continued.

"Twenty thousand sealed copies of my last testament will be opened and published in all parts of the country immediately after my death or disappearance for twenty-four hours. That testament is the secret process for manufacturing gold."

For an instant of tense silence he studied the leader of the Chosen Clique. Then he cried triumphantly: "My death will destroy the world you want to rule. Your only hope of wealth and power depends on my safety and willingness to overlook your pretentious plotting. That is your choice."

Twice Ebets thrust his hand toward the table, and twice he drew it back, while the Master watched him with scornful unconcern.

Then the leader of the Chosen Clique picked up his watch and returned it to his pocket. In a quandary he took a few steps across the cabin.

"How do I know you're telling the truth?" he asked abruptly.

"You don't," returned the Master. "Nor will you till after I'm dead; but you're convinced that I am, and wisely so."

Ebets asked another question, "Suppose I return you to Ransler Castle unharmed, will members of the Chosen Clique and their followers retain their wealth and position on the Upper Level?"

"Promises are unnecessary," replied the Master swiftly. "It is to my interest as well as theirs to hold the organization of the System intact. No one will be punished. But you must do more than take me back unharmed. You must call the Chosen Clique together at once and set about subduing the revolt on the Lower Level also!"

Ebets nodded thoughtfully.

"You're still the Master," he said at last, with sullen admiration. "I'll follow your orders."

He stepped to the door of the after saloon and called in his bravos and the captain of the ship. To the latter he gave a brief command. The bravos he directed to release the prisoners. He himself carefully detached the push button and cord from the floor, and locked the trap door to prevent its opening accidentally.

Dawn was breaking when the helicopter settled down once more on the roof of Ransler Castle. As if nothing unusual had happened, the Master ordered the plane to be held in readiness to take off in case of emergency. Ebets, Dr. Edgerton, and Jimmy accompanied him into his sanctum. The two deaf-and-dumb secretaries looked at the little party curiously; but it was apparent that no disturbance had been caused by the ephemeral kidnapping.

Ebets, after receiving a few instructions, hurried from the roof to call the Chosen Clique into session and set in motion all the machinery at their command to undo the work of revolution in which they had been engaged for months.

When he had gone, Dr. Edgerton and Jimmy silently delivered their copies of the report from the Senior Commissioner.

"You'll hear from me later in the day," said the Master, dismissing them. "You, Manse, I want to talk to in particular."

Jimmy did not answer. He and the doctor descended to their rooms, took off their clothing, and went to bed.

It was nearly noon when Jimmy awoke. He slipped into a lounging robe and hastened into the doctor's room. The older man, already dressed, was listening to radio reports of the news.

The Master's victory over the Chosen Clique was beginning to manifest itself in the stock market. Prices were soaring. The powerful financial group that had allied itself against him was trying to buy back stocks it had been furiously selling for months.

With astonishing rapidity the attitude toward the Master on the Upper Level was changing. Could Dr. Edgerton and Jimmy have seen his two secretaries, receiving and answering messages from the financial district and all the big cities in the country, they would have realized more fully how great this change already was.

The tenor of every incoming dispatch was the same. Each expressed eagerness to assist in stamping out the embers of revolt. The most anxious solicitude concerning the Master's wishes came from those who had secretly been most active in plotting his downfall.

Every reply he sent back sounded a note of supreme confidence. In no case did he give the slightest intimation that he knew he was answering one of those who twenty-four hours previously had determined to destroy him and rule in his stead.

Every report on the radio reflected the shift from sedition to support of the System. Dr. Edgerton greeted this transformation with enthusiastic satisfaction. It was what he had expected. But to Jimmy it seemed an unwholesome victory for the corrupt life of the Upper Level. He thought with horror of what he had heard about his father. The quiet, sane environment of New City suddenly seemed far away.

The doctor tried to lift the young man out of his moody meditation by commenting on the cheerful turn affairs had taken, but Jimmy showed little interest in the general news. He wanted definite information about Miriam, and grew uneasy and restless. Finally he announced, "I'm going down to the Lower Level. If the danger of revolution is over, the danger in my seeing Miriam has passed."

Dr. Edgerton opposed this conclusion vigorously.

"You must still be cautious, my boy," he insisted. "This is no time to take a chance."

But Jimmy's anxiety to see Miriam hardened into stubborn resolution to seek her on the Lower Level. Dr. Edgerton's objections were useless.

"Before you go," he said at last, "let me try to learn something about conditions there."

To this compromise Jimmy grudgingly consented, and the doctor left him with a farewell admonition, "Don't get dressed until I come back. You'll have an excuse to refuse admission to callers. And don't tell anyone I'm not here with you."

Nearly an hour passed before he returned. The instant he entered the room he asked if anyone had called or phoned. When informed that no one had, he drew a breath of relief and sat down.

"It's a good thing you didn't try to go down to the Lower Level," he began, "For weeks no one has been allowed to pass through the gates either way, without a special permit from the Master. Had you tried, you would have been held for questioning."

"I'm sick of all this mystery and deceit," cried Jimmy, irritably.

"Don't let nerves interfere with common sense," urged the doctor, shortly. "You're going to need all the discretion you have. I saw Georgette Graylor for a moment at the entrance. She'll meet you in half an hour. Walk one block north and three blocks west, and you'll find her. Act as if the meeting were accidental—in case you're observed. After you talk with her come directly back here."

He chose this moment to tell Jimmy of the deception Georgette had practiced on Vivian Ransler, and explained the reason for her affectionate greeting when they discovered her in Bromwell's arms. His wisdom in not telling this before was confirmed by Jimmy's anger.

"Your temper is unjust," interrupted the doctor with a vehemence he seldom showed in addressing the young man. "Regardless of her purpose, what she did protected Miriam at a critical time. She's a courageous girl; and she's in a dangerous position on account of you. Don't seem ungrateful to her, or she may not tell you things you'd like to know."

Jimmy, on his way to meet Georgette, thought over what the doctor had said. For the first time he understood the position she was in.

She met him with an air of indifference, but as they walked along together said quickly. "It's better not to show I'm glad to see you, Jimmy. Someone may be watching us. That wouldn't make much difference to you, but to me it might mean a lot."

She was not the same buoyant, vivacious Georgette.

Worry and restraint had drawn little wrinkles about her eyes, and hardened their expression. But her courage had not deserted her.

"I've been subjected to every form of humiliation," she continued bitterly. "I'm little more than a servant to Vivian Ransler. I can't stand it much longer, and," with suppressed anger, "I won't."

She bit her lip to hold back what threatened to become a tirade of pent up accusation.

"Take it easy," said Jimmy gently. "Tell me all you can about Miriam. How is she? Where is she? What's she doing?"

Georgette stared at him in astonishment.

"You don't know?" she exclaimed.

He shook his head impatiently.

For a moment she hesitated, and then said bluntly, "Miriam's the real leader of the revolution on the Lower Level. Yes, it is astonishing. I never supposed she had great initiative, but the whole underworld looks up to her as a kind of Joan of Arc. She has been in half a dozen cities organizing the army of girls. Now she's back here again in active command of the original corps of more than two hundred thousand."

Jimmy was dumbfounded.

"Have you seen her?" he cried.

Georgette shook her head.

"But I've had access to Vivian Ransler's private reports from spies in Miriam's own guard of honor. They say that the army of girls will attack the Upper Level this very week."

"The Chosen Clique has resumed allegiance to the System," protested Jimmy. "The revolution is over."

"You think so?" she queried.

"Of course I do," he asserted.

"Why? Nothing has happened to change the hatred felt for the Master by the unemployed and thousands of workers. Why should the army of girls be less determined to destroy the Upper Level today than it was yesterday?"

"The Chosen Clique will prevent an attack."

"If it can," murmured Georgette.

Jimmy looked at her with growing trepidation.

"You must find out exactly where Miriam is—how I can get word to her!"

In his earnestness he gripped her arm so tightly that she gave a little cry of pain.

"I can only promise I'll try," she said.

"Where can I see you tonight?" he asked anxiously.

Georgette thought a moment.

"The Ransler Household Association is giving a ball at the Uptown Terpsichorium. I'll go there—not before eleven o'clock; maybe later. It's not far from here. Ask me for a dance, and I'll let you know what I've been able to find out."

They separated and each returned to Ransler Castle alone.

Dr. Edgerton was nervously pacing up and down his room.

"I thought you'd never get back," he exclaimed. "The Master wants to see us. I sent word we were dressing, but would be up in a few moments."

In the outer room of the central penthouse they were directed to take places at the end of a long line of financiers, managers of industry, officers of protective corps and others who were being admitted to the sanctum one by one. Each went in alone. At the end of a minute or two he emerged, and the next in line hurried into the presence of the Master.

The atmosphere was charged with repressed excitement. Jimmy's place was just ahead of Dr. Edgerton. He realized as the line rapidly dwindled away in front of him, while maintaining its length by the tailing on of newcomers continually arriving, that the great organization of the System was working under pressure. When he reached the door two guards hurried him through and closed it, keeping the doctor outside to wait his turn.

The Master stood facing the entrance, alert, but looking fatigued. He wasted no words in coming to the purpose of this meeting, but said abruptly, "You misunderstand the meaning of what Ebets said about your father. Two bodyguards I chose to protect him got an inkling of his discovery. They assassinated him because he would not tell them the secret he had entrusted to my care and promised to disclose to no one else."

He looked straight into the young man's eyes, and continued in a voice that sounded old and tired. "I wanted you to know this. You have the right to call on me for any service within my power."

With sudden crispness, he added, "That's all, my boy."

Almost before Jimmy was aware that he had moved, he found himself outside the sanctum and saw the doctor enter. Dazed he stood looking at the closed door.

On the other side of it, Dr. Edgerton listened with amazement to what the Master was telling him.

"Impossible!" he interrupted.

"Doctor," replied the Master smoothly. "I've pointed out the weakness of you intellectuals in misjudging the future. The Chosen Clique can easily quell revolt on the Upper Level, but to prevent revolution on the Lower Level now, is a different matter."

"Bribes ought to be powerful there," declared the doctor.

"Not even with the criminal gangs that have turned revolutionary. They think they can get more by looting than by bargaining."

Dr. Edgerton frowned.

"If they stood in the open alone," the Master went on, "the System could quickly crush these outlaws. But they hide behind the army of girls, whose idealism has become a religion; their leader, a goddess. Our protective corps may have to shoot these girls down like rats."

The doctor shook his head uneasily; and the Master concluded, "To capture their leader before a shot is fired and hold her as a hostage is the plan of the Chosen Clique. Tell it to no one; but if it fails, bring Manse here to me at once."

CHAPTER TWENTY-ONE

AS the afternoon wore away the completeness of the Master's victory on the Upper Level became evident to all. The up rush of the stock market proclaimed his triumph over the attempt to gain the gold supply. Miscarriage of this fundamental purpose of the Chosen Clique instantly smothered within the inner circle all incentive to revolt.

Traitorous leaders and their cohorts accepted defeat with hypocritical enthusiasm, intended to simulate innocence of having had anything to do with fomenting rebellion. Worried multimillionaires, financiers, managers of industry hailed one another like steadfast comrades in a hard-won cause, lauded the Master in fulsome words and vigorously condemned opposition to his rule.

Protective corps that for weeks had held themselves suspiciously aloof, waiting for their employers to order them which side to take, assumed a friendly attitude. The members fraternized in harmonious loyalty to the System.

Hundreds of spies of the Chosen Clique, long established in important positions to betray the Master at the crucial moment, suddenly became martinets in carrying out his instructions. As evening drew on it would have been difficult to find on all the Upper Level throughout the country a soul hardy enough to denounce his dictatorship. The attempt to overthrow him was belittled as a flash of political fever that had passed and left the body politic healthier than it was before.

That seeds of revolution could germinate into sedition on the Lower Level, without the cultivation of Upper Level leadership, seemed inconceivable. Authoritative political judgment, saturated with Machiavellian precepts, held that the extent of popular uprisings depended on instigation from above, not below.

But the supreme council of the Chosen Clique, trying to annihilate its Frankenstein of rebellion that stalked boldly through the restless millions of Lower Level population, grew fearful as succeeding reports came in.

Municipal guards at all entrances to the Upper Level were doubled. The protective corps of each member of the inner circle was ordered to report for mass duty.

The System building in the financial district, where vaults of the Central Bank held billions of gold, was patrolled by hundreds of secret agents recalled from service on the Lower Level, and defended by a picked detachment of municipal troops, equipped with the most modern weapons of defense and attack.

Ransler Castle, and the grounds surrounding it, swarmed with male bravos of the Master and female bravos of Vivian Ransler.

Down on the Lower Level Edward Bane and other disseminators of idealist propaganda were inflaming crowds of discontented, sullen men to the pitch of fury. They charged that the Chosen Clique had surrendered without a struggle—had sold them out when victory was within reach. Would they submit to this treachery?

Roars of angry negation greeted the question. Members of criminal bands, mixing with the unemployed, urged sabotage in machine shops and the bombing of industrial plants. Others stole into half deserted residence districts, tried to set fire to the homes of workers and spread rumors that incendiaries hired by the System planned a conflagration to consume the underworld.

No discipline prevailed, except in the corps of two hundred thousand girls commanded by Miriam Estley. These intensively trained combatants were under arms and ready to storm the Upper Level at a moment's notice. In a score of cities similar corps prepared to begin the attack simultaneously.

At staff headquarters Miriam, her aides, and idealists like Bane—who had recruited groups from workers, artists and students for the irregular army of men—impatiently waited for the signal. Uplifted by aspirations to found a new democracy, they forgot that envy, hatred, and greed for plunder alone stirred thousands of those most eager for revolution.

In the background a criminal rabble cunningly curbed its ferocity, counting on victorious attack by the corps of girls to open a way for the mob to unrestrained pillage. Once let loose amid the wealth and luxury of the Upper Level, it would observe no bounds in brutal excesses of depravity. No feminist army would be able to hold in check a raging proletariat whipped on to vandalism by criminals. The country would plunge into helpless disorder beyond the control of any government.

The council of the Chosen Clique perceived this menace with growing alarm. At all hazards the thrust by the army of girls must be delayed to allow time to incite dissension in the different revolutionary groups. Ebets and his colleagues, with the help of the Master, directed every resource of the System to this end.

When darkness fell Miriam left her staff headquarters, established in a community center far out on the West Side, to make a final tour of inspection. Communiqués from other cities informed her that the defection of the Chosen Clique had raised no obstacle there to preparations for the uprising.

With four members of her guard of honor she rode in an armored car, preceded by a small scout car and followed by another. It was not yet seven o'clock when she set out, leaving word with her aides. Bane and other members of the Board of Strategy, that she would be back by ten for the last conference before declaring civil war by ordering the attack.

The local plan of campaign contemplated advance at the same instant against a dozen gates far apart on the northern, western and southern edges of the Upper Level. The purpose was to draw defenders from the heart of the city, while storm troops of girls hurried under cover of darkness to the real objectives, the Jackson Boulevard entrance at LaSalle Street in the financial district, and the Oak Street entrance at Lake Shore Drive on the near North Side. If entry was affected at these two points, defenders of the outlying gates could be cut down separately from behind, and the upper world would be at the mercy of the invaders.

Except the corps of girls, the Lower Level forces were ill equipped to carry on a siege. Members of the Chosen Clique had undertaken to provide adequate munitions. Now that they had resumed allegiance to the Master, not only were sources of supplies shut off, but the expected support of thousands of trained bravos on the Upper Level was suddenly turned against the Lower Level army.

No one knew better than Miriam the terrific blow this dealt the insurrection. No one knew better the danger to the revolutionary cause in delaying the attack. She determined to order it at midnight or shortly thereafter at the latest.

With a heavy heart she drove from one to another of the outlying gates chosen for assault. Everywhere she met enthusiasm. The battalions of well drilled girls and the irregular companies of men idealists had no comprehension of what the desertion of the Chosen Clique meant. Their ardor was unaffected, and they looked forward to victory with the same supreme confidence in Miriam's leadership that had been their inspiration through weeks of excited anticipation.

Valiantly she greeted the officers at each base of attack with words of commendation on the high morale of their commands, and hastened on to the next stop for inspection. But a terrible sadness began to engulf her. No doubt of the justness of her leadership and the nobility of the cause for which they were about to fight assailed her mind; it was the responsibility of ordering these light-hearted girls and high-minded men into the horrors of warfare that overwhelmed her. Suddenly she realized that this impending civil war, regardless of the moral rectitude and humane eagerness that inspired it, was like all other projected wars—a monstrous prospectus for wholesale murder.

She tried to steel her mind against this bitter conclusion. She thought of Jimmy and her love for him.

Her efforts to discover his whereabouts had been futile. If the leaders of the Chosen Clique knew, they had withheld their information to stimulate hatred for the Master.

The disappearance of Jimmy and Dr. Edgerton from the Upper Level could only mean they had been assassinated by the monster who ruled as dictator. Hot hatred of the Master and the System flamed in her heart.

Completing her inspection of the twelve outlying gates, Miriam ordered a return to headquarters. On the way, one of her guard of honor suggested driving to the Jackson Boulevard gate at LaSalle Street to examine the protection from defensive fire offered by the shelter of the upper drive. No detachment of Lower Level forces was at this gate. Not even a sentry was stationed there, in order to make the most of the element of surprise.

It was only nine o'clock, but Miriam hesitated to deviate from her schedule. Another of her quartet of guards decried the suggestion as too dangerous to follow.

The strange pride of a commander that leads to unwise action in order to avoid appearance of what might seem to be a want of courage, touched Miriam to the quick. She gave a brief command to the chauffeur, and the heavy car swung eastward. At the western edge of the Upper Level it turned in under the Jackson Boulevard upper drive, and moved more slowly in the dark Lower Level thoroughfare toward the LaSalle Street gate.

CHAPTER TWENTY-TWO

JIMMY and Dr. Edgerton had dined in their apartment. The former restlessly waited for the time to keep his appointment with Georgette. Again he told the doctor, thoughtful and unresponsive, the information she had given him, and added confidently:

"If she can only learn exactly where Miriam is. I'll find a way to see her."

When he and Dr. Edgerton reached the Uptown Terpsichorium at eleven o'clock the festivities of the Ransler Household Employees Association had begun to take on the semblance of an orgy of victory.

From the roof of the square, glassite building the ballroom hung suspended by cables, looking like a great dirigible floating in its hangar. A huge shell of resonant wood, it quivered with the barbaric beat of the music in the same maddening rhythm that incited sensuous undulations in the dancers.

To prevent deadening the vibrations, a space of several inches separated the ballroom from the floor that surrounded it like a landing platform. On this, coat and cloak rooms, rest rooms, lounges and intimate alcoves provided convenience, comfort and luxury. To enter the ballroom through one of the broad doorways it was necessary to step over the intervening crevice. Instantly the entrant felt, like an electric shock, the strange vitality of a new atmosphere.

When Jimmy and the doctor arrived, the climax of emotion was already rising toward a culmination in utter abandon that would come in the early morning hours. Two orchestras crowded one dance upon another with hardly a moment's intermission. The air was warm with the glow of a thousand young bodies, throbbing with pleasure. The ballroom vibrated with increasing intensity to the thick, deep notes of cello and bass, and the incessant thumping of tom-toms.

Jimmy, with the doctor close beside him, sauntered about in search of Georgette. She was nowhere to be found. They concluded she had not yet arrived, and took a position just inside the entrance of the building to wait for her. It was long after eleven o'clock before she made her appearance.

She came in breathless, and walked past them with a look that warned against any greeting. They followed her into one of the nooks so dimly lighted that recognition of anyone within it from the outside was almost impossible. They waited for her to speak.

Her eyes wide with excitement, full of terror.

"They've captured Miriam!" she gasped.

"What!" cried Jimmy.

She looked at him steadily, trying to control her rapid breathing.

"I've seen her," she whispered, "at a distance. They want to keep the place she's held a prisoner secret. She's locked in a room of Vivian Ransler's apartment on the seventh floor. Two of her own guard of honor betrayed her. They and a half a dozen of Vivian's other spies are on duty in the suite. Outside the corridors are filled with Ebets' bravos."

In a trembling voice she added swiftly, "Oh, Jimmy, the Chosen Clique has sent word to her staff that at the first outbreak of violence against the Upper Level they'll hang her as a warning to traitors."

For a moment all three stood speechless. Tears were streaming from Georgette's eyes.

"They can't do that!" Jimmy burst out in a frenzy. "It's too horrible!"

Dr. Edgerton moved uneasily, but said nothing.

"Georgette," cried Jimmy, "you're the only one who can do anything." He seized her wrist fiercely. "Find a way to get her out of that room."

She remained passive in his painful grip until Dr. Edgerton brought him to his senses by taking his arm.

"There's nothing I can do," Georgette said humbly. "I can't return to Ransler Castle. I'm suspected. I must hide until I can get back to the Lower Level. I may be followed now."

She left them as hurriedly as she had come.

Jimmy turned to Dr. Edgerton.

"I'm going to see the Master at once," he declared. "Don't try to tell me what to do."

They hastened back to Ransler Castle.

As they stood waiting for the elevator to carry them up to the penthouse, the doctor glanced at his watch. It was a quarter of twelve.

The descending elevator stopped, the door opened, and Vivian Ransler emerged.

"Jimmy," she exclaimed, delighted. "Jimmy, I'm so glad to see you back again." She held out her hand.

The young man hesitated an instant, and then to Dr. Edgerton's amazement seized her hand effusively.

"I'm glad to be back," he said.

"Where on earth have you been this evening?" she asked curiously.

He told her, and she laughed rather scornfully.

"That's no sort of party for you to go to," she deprecated. "If you want to dance, come into the ballroom with me. There's no crowd there. You'll have better music, too, and I think as good a partner."

Her eyes flashed with bold desire to possess him.

"I've something important to do first," he replied.

"How long will it take?"

"Five or ten minutes. Twenty at the outside."

"I'll wait for you," she promised, and turned away, with hardly a glance at Dr. Edgerton.

The two men entered the elevator, and were carried up to the roof.

They were instantly admitted to the sanctum of the Master. He was alone, exhausted by the drain on his nervous force and by loss of sleep.

Jimmy, with no attempt to restrain his emotion, demanded that Miriam be released immediately. In a tumult of words he emphasized the danger of irresponsible attack on the Upper Level, the injustice of holding her accountable if it occurred, the infamy of the threat of execution.

He told of their relations, their hope for future happiness, her character, her beauty, her sincerity, her courage.

"Today," he cried, "you told me to call on you for any service within your power. I call on you now. Set Miriam free and let me take her away from here. That's the only service I'll ever ask."

The Master listened without a word of interruption. He took a few steps across the floor in silence, his head bowed. Suddenly he straightened up with the energy of decision.

"You ask me to order Miriam Estley's release." He hesitated. "My boy, if I did that it would be a sorry service. She would be assassinated instantly."

CHAPTER TWENTY-THREE

DR. EDGERTON was quick to grasp the truth of what the Master said. The Chosen Clique would never let Miriam go. What better scapegoat to load with ignominy and blame for the uprising? There must be no trial to megaphone the traitorous perfidy of many a multimillionaire unsuspected by the public on the Upper Level.

She knew who the powerful figures were that had been in collusion with the Lower Level. For that knowledge she must pay with her life. The less certain the success of the revolution, the more surely must she pay; for resumption of unopposed control by the System might force her to testify to the treason of personages in high places, who now disavowed and were trying to conceal their disloyalty.

Jimmy sank into a chair, and pressed his hands to his head.

But no uncertainty disturbed the Master. Clearly he foresaw why the Chosen Clique would never obey his order to set Miriam free, if he issued it. He had lost, for a time at least, his prerogative of absolute authority.

The knowledge that traitors who had plotted his downfall, although defeated, would still dare to oppose his will enraged him. He strode to the desk at which his deaf-and-dumb secretaries sat, and worked his dexterous fingers with lightning facility.

Dr. Edgerton watched him in fascinated admiration.

One secretary hastily typed directions on slips of paper. The Master signed one of these, and the secretary hurried with it through the tunnel that led to the landing table, where the helicopter plane stood ready to take off.

The other secretary opened a cabinet, put several articles into his pocket, and brought forward three small needle-guns. One he gave to Dr. Edgerton, another to the still confused Jimmy, the third he strapped into the palm of his own left hand.

The Master leaned over Jimmy, like a hypnotist exerting control, and concentrated all the power of his indomitable personality on the young man.

"Rescue Miriam Estley," he commanded. "Bring her here. My secretary will show the way."

Already the secretary had opened the door in the floor. He, Jimmy, and Dr. Edgerton ran down the steps into the room beneath the sanctum, and thence began a long descent down circular stairways and through tortuous passages that honeycombed the thick walls.

At regular intervals the secretary referred to a small diagram in a flash from his electric torch.

They came to the seventh floor, and proceeded along a narrow, level passageway in single file. Intermittent flashes from the torch in front gave Dr. Edgerton, who was last, glimpses of the walls on each side. He reached out and touched first one and then the other. They were cold steel. Beneath his feet a thick padding of felt muffled the heaviest footstep.

Abruptly the secretary halted, and closely examined the left-hand wall in the light of the torch. He found the mark of identification he sought.

Reaching past Jimmy, he seized Dr. Edgerton's wrist and pulled him forward. Into the doctor's hand he thrust a typewritten slip of paper, and turned the light upon it.

"Dr. Edgerton is to go in first," the doctor read. "He must remember that Miriam Estley thinks that he and Manse are dead."

The secretary began to manipulate a mechanism in the wall. He extinguished the torch, and they stood in impenetrable darkness. In Jimmy's ears the blood was pounding furiously.

A vertical thread of light slit the back wall. It widened quickly, as a panel noiselessly slid aside, opening the way into the room that held Miriam a prisoner.

Dr. Edgerton stepped through the aperture.

From an adjoining room, into which the door was wide open, came a woman's voice. "Her army will never begin an attack that will cause her execution."

"But a band of criminals will," replied a second feminine voice. "The Chosen Clique has seen to that."

Laughter in low tones followed.

Dr. Edgerton looked down at the needle-gun in his right palm. "Will I be called upon to kill these women guards?" he thought in horror.

Where was Miriam?

His eyes swept the room before him, and suddenly he saw her. Only her feet were visible. Bound together with a heavy rope they lay on the end of a chaise longue, the back of which was toward him.

Thrusting his hand behind him he caught the arm of the secretary and drew him through the panel. He pointed out where Miriam lay, and indicated that guards were in the adjoining room.

Jimmy, who had followed the secretary, took in the situation at the same moment.

What if Miriam, thinking that he had been assassinated, should cry out in surprise at first sight of him?

Dr. Edgerton and the secretary took up positions on each side of the panel, with guns pointed at the open doorway into the adjoining room. Jimmy stole forward on tiptoe toward the chaise-longue on which Miriam lay.

The doctor and the secretary did not dare turn their eyes from the doorway to watch him. They waited, breathless, expecting every instant to hear some sound that would give the alarm, and bring the guards rushing in upon them.

But nothing disturbed the silence, except the low murmur of voices in the adjoining room.

Suddenly Jimmy was back within range of their vision, carrying Miriam. She was unconscious from the effects of gas or some drug used to consummate her capture.

The snap of nervous tension started tears of relief down Dr. Edgerton's cheeks. The secretary's eyes glistened with the satisfaction of efficient performance.

He backed quickly through the panel into the secret passage. Jimmy, with Miriam in his arms, followed, and Dr. Edgerton brought up the rear. The panel quietly closed, and they stood huddled together in the darkness while the secretary locked it fast.

Return to the sanctum was accomplished speedily. Jimmy laid Miriam on a lounge, and cut the ropes that tied her ankles and wrists. She was breathing regularly, but was still unconscious.

A house intern, called by the Master in case of need, made a rapid examination.

"Gas," he said, quietly. "Another half hour will bring her to. No harmful effects will follow.

He left the sanctum, and the Master watched his retreating form through the Univision partition. The instant it disappeared in the darkness outside the penthouse he turned to Jimmy.

"Carry her aboard the helicopter at once," he directed energetically.

Jimmy picked Miriam up in his arms, and accompanied by Dr. Edgerton, hastened to the plane on the unlighted landing-table. He lifted her aboard with the help of the steward and followed himself.

"Goodbye, my boy," called Dr. Edgerton in a low voice.

"Aren't you coming, too?" gasped the young man in surprise.

"I'm going to stay with the Master," answered the doctor shortly.

He turned away as the ship rose in the darkness.

The Master stood gazing through the eastern wall of his sanctum at the slowly moving light that marked the course of the helicopter as it swung southward over the lake. Surprised at Dr. Edgerton's return, he looked at him with a friendliness in his eyes the doctor had never seen there before.

"It's dangerous to remain with me," he said, rather sadly.

He stepped to his desk, lifted a section of the top, and sat down before the private ray-phone concealed inside. A moment later he was telling the Senior Commissioner at New City to meet the helicopter plane.

As he closed the desk after finishing his conversation, and faced the doctor, the low rumble of a terrific explosion came to their ears. A moment of silence followed, and then another detonation made the building vibrate.

"They're bombing the Upper Level," cried Dr. Edgerton.

The Master unlocked a drawer and took out a single, folded sheet of paper. He held it toward the doctor.

"If anything happens to me," he said impressively. "I count on you to carry out these directions."

Dr. Edgerton slipped the paper into an inside pocket with a gloomy misgiving he tried to hide from himself.

The Master pointed into the deep, open drawer at five heavy, electric switches, each with a number stamped into its handle.

"The last resort," he said, as another distant explosion made the floor of the sanctum tremble.

A machine of communication began to operate rapidly. One of the secretaries pulled out a printed message and brought it to the Master. He glanced at it swiftly, and passed it on to the doctor, with the laconic exclamation. "From the Chosen Clique!"

Dr. Edgerton scanned the few lines: "Two bombing planes are over the lake. The pilots know the channel to the roof of Ransler Castle. Close it quick, and all other channels through the net-ray protection."

Before the doctor had finished reading, the Master, by one of the machines in front of his secretaries, had given the command instantly to close all the air channels. His anger was apparent. He was being forced to take orders from the Chosen Clique.

They hurried to the eastern wall of the sanctum, and stared out into the blackness over the lake. A blotch of flame burst forth high in the air. The roar of an explosion followed immediately. The flame fell like a meteor.

Not a moment too soon had the Bureau of Aerial Defense executed the command to close the channel. The first bombing plane had touched the net-ray protection and exploded instantly.

Before the blazing wreckage plunged to extinction in the lake, the second bomber, unable to change its course in time, met the same fate.

The Master went back to his desk, and dropped into a chair beside it. He expected another message from the Chosen Clique. He picked up a long, heavy, gold handled paper cutter, like a dagger, and stabbed nervously into the blotter under his hand.

Dr. Edgerton felt sure the escape of Miriam must have been discovered by this time. It seemed impossible that the Master could go unsuspected of having spirited her out of the closely watched room in which she had been a prisoner.

Looking through the partition into the outer office, where a dozen picked members of the Master's bodyguard were on duty, he saw the door from the dark roof suddenly flung open.

Vivian Ransler stood on the threshold. But only for an instant.

Straight to the sanctum she ran, and knocked at the locked door. No guard had the hardihood to stop the daughter of the Master.

Her face was flushed, but whether from excess of some dissipation, or with anger, Dr. Edgerton was not sure.

The Master hesitated a moment. Then, with a sigh of annoyance, he pressed the button that allowed the door to be opened. She rushed to his side where he sat by his desk. The presence of Dr. Edgerton and the secretaries she ignored.

"What have you done with her?" she demanded peremptorily.

He looked surprised at her tone.

"Whom?" he asked quietly.

"Oh," snapped Vivian, with uncontrolled impatience, "don't try to treat me like a fool!"

The paper cutter with which the Master had been digging into the blotter, dropped from his hand.

"Sit down, Vivian," he ordered sharply. "Dr. Edgerton is present, and you are not yourself."

But she did not move from her place close beside him, although she looked toward Dr. Edgerton for the first time.

"Where's Jimmy Manse?" she cried hotly.

The doctor made no answer.

"He tricked me into waiting for him away from the room in which Miriam Estley was prisoner!"

Her blazing eyes swept back to the Master.

"You told him to do that! No one but you could have arranged her escape!"

"Listen, Vivian," he commanded. "You're mistaken."

"I don't believe you!" she interrupted insolently.

A swift contraction of the Master's forehead deepened the lines between his eyes, but his hands remained quietly folded in his lap. In a low voice he said with careful distinctness, "The Chosen Clique would have hanged her—a foolish design to smash the rebellion that would have made matters worse. It was better to get her out of the city, and spread the report that she had accepted a bribe and deserted her followers."

"Jimmy Manse did take part in rescuing her, then," she persisted. "Where is he now?"

"He has taken her away," answered the Master calmly. "A disturbing element has been removed."

The whole truth flashed upon her. For a moment she was speechless. Then she burst into a fury of intolerant vituperation.

"That's the girl he loved all the time!" she cried, with rising hysteria. "What a fool I've let him make of me!"

Her rage against herself turned upon the Master.

"You knew it!" she fairly shrieked. "And you helped them get away together!"

She snatched the paper cutter from the desk, and plunged it into his breast.

So unexpected was the blow that he made no resistance. Feebly he lifted one hand for an instant, as if in protest. It dropped limply to his side, and his head fell forward.

Vivian, insane with anger, threw the bloody, golden knife at Dr. Edgerton's feet, dashed from the sanctum, passed the guards in the outer room, and rushed into the darkness on the roof outside.

At the same moment the crashing rattle of distant machine gun fire proclaimed that attack against the Upper Level had begun in earnest.

CHAPTER TWENTY-FOUR

FOR a moment the inertia of horror held Dr. Edgerton immovable. Hardly conscious of hearing the machine gun fire in the distance, he stared at the figure slumped down in the chair beside the desk.

Then the power to act returned, and he sprang to the victim of Vivian's frenzy.

The Master was coughing weakly. With every spasm his head rolled helplessly, and blood drooled from his mouth.

The doctor signed to the secretaries to carry the wounded man to the lounge, and rushed to the door.

"Get an intern, quick!" he ordered the officers of the guard outside. "Let no one else in! The Master's ill."

He closed the door, and ran to the lounge.

One of the secretaries was bathing the Master's face with a wet towel.

Gently Dr. Edgerton unbuttoned the bloody waistcoat and shirt to lay bare the wound for examination.

The Master opened his eyes feebly. His brow puckered, and he made an effort to speak; but a fit of coughing, accompanied by a gush of blood, choked him. He lifted a hand and touched the doctor, who was bending over him, on the right breast.

Dr. Edgerton nodded encouragingly.

"The intern will be here in a minute," he promised.

But the wounded man frowned wearily, and pressed his hand against the other's coat. Sudden interpretation of what that gesture meant enlightened the doctor. He pulled from his pocket the folded paper the Master had given him.

"It's all right," he soothed. "I've got it."

The Master smiled faintly, and instantly relapsed into unconsciousness.

One of the secretaries seized Dr. Edgerton's arm and pointed to the door. Outside waited the house physician who had attended Miriam. Dr. Edgerton motioned to let him in.

He advanced briskly; but when he saw the Master, lying unconscious and gasping for breath, his manner changed. He shook his head gravely. The briefest examination of the small, external wound above the heart told the shocking truth. The lung had been transfixed, the heart probably pierced.

He turned away.

"Only a miracle can save him," he declared, scrutinizing Dr. Edgerton keenly.

The machine gun firing in the distance became continuous. In the physician's eyes Dr. Edgerton read suspicion and a rising fear.

"Stay here," he said, authoritatively. "Make him as comfortable as you can. No one else will be allowed to enter."

Heavy responsibility for a decision he had made oppressed him.

He looked through the univision partition at the guards, alert and apparently undisturbed. They were gazing out through the walls into the darkness.

On a scrap of paper he wrote a brief order, "Keep everyone off the roof," and gave it to one of the secretaries to transmit to the commanding officer.

Then he drew a chair to the lounge, and sat down beside the Master. He glanced at his watch. It was after one o'clock.

A burst of louder firing announced attack at the Oak Street entrance. Heavy artillery for deadly gas warfare rumbled by Ransler Castle at double-quick.

To the general public on the Upper Level, quieted into belief that the danger of revolution was over, the first firing had seemed little cause for trepidation. It was thought to be a last futile effort of malcontents, too fanatical to realize that defection of the Chosen Clique had made their cause a hopeless one.

But scorn for the ineffectiveness of the underworld in action requiring organization and methodical execution, became tempered with terror of the undisciplined power of mob violence.

At the Uptown Terpsichorium, where little more than an hour before hundreds of young couples plunged into pleasure without a care, the ardor of the dancers waned. Messengers arrived with orders for those who held positions of responsibility in the System, to report for duty immediately. The festivities lost the semblance of an orgy of victory.

On the Lower Level, except for the discipline that controlled the corps of girls, disorder and confusion ran riot.

Bands of criminals, fearful that the capture of Miriam Estley might crush the hot spirit of revolution and prevent opportunity for plunder, had exploded bombs and spread rumors that she had escaped, that the Upper Level was in panic.

In the residence quarters they roused the populace, cried the alarm that war had been declared, that the army of girls was sweeping all before it throughout the country.

The masses poured into the streets. Section after section vomited its mob into the crowd rushing toward the area of the Upper Level.

No one high in command ordered the attack, but at one after another of the twelve selected gates it began spontaneously. At each the girl officers supposed the order had been sent out from general headquarters, but failed to reach them. Not daring to risk by hesitation weakening the effect of concerted action, they led the onslaughts.

The Board of Strategy was helpless. Revolution had burst beyond control. Hurried messages conveyed to distant cities the news that war had begun.

Storm troops of girls rushed to the gate in the financial district and the gate on the near North Side. Their immediate officers shouldered the responsibility for carrying out the comprehensive plan of attack without orders.

Workers, the unemployed, artists, students, criminals, both men and women, caught up anything that would serve as a weapon, and swarmed into the center of the city under the upper drives, a self-inflaming rabble.

A hunt for Lower Level sympathizers with the System began. Street sweepers, scavengers, watchmen, petty clerks, were roped and dragged to death through the streets, or strung up to girders supporting the upper drives. To be suspected, was to be accused; to be accused, was to be guilty; to be guilty, was to be murdered without mercy.

At the twelve outlying gates the attacking battalions of girls met perfectly organized defense. Machine guns and waves of gas mowed down assault after assault.

Lack of equipment to care for the wounded made the scene at each gate a nightmare of hell. Young girls, not out of their teens, were shot down on the narrow stairways like lambs in a shambles. The steps grew slippery with blood. Young bodies, bullet-torn and trampled underfoot, lay in piles.

Hundreds, terribly wounded, screaming in agony, tried to drag themselves on hands and knees away from the carnage.

Suddenly above the noise and tumult of wholesale murder, the shrill screeching of the gigantic siren on top of the System building made itself heard. Over and over again it ran its bloodcurdling gamut. Another siren on the far North Side hurled forth ear-splitting shrieks; and then another on the West Side, and another far out near the southern edge of the Upper Level.

A strange lull swept over the fighting. The bravo at his machine gun stayed his fire; the young girl officer about to order an assault withheld the command; the criminal ready to hurl a bomb, stood poised.

With the abruptness of a light suddenly extinguished, the screams of the sirens ceased. Then, in that moment of stillness, a mighty voice split the very clouds. It came from the Orpheus Pagoda of amplifiers on the lake front, from the Magnavox on the System building, from the lighthouses in the harbor, from the powerful enunciators in every park and auditorium, from every private loudspeaker on the Upper Level and the Lower Level alike.

The same voice, amplified millions of times, burst forth from every vocal machine at once with such tremendous magnitude of sound that it smote the ears of every resident, high and low, indoors and out, and rolled away for miles over the quiet waters of the lake.

The same words, at the same instant, thundered through the skyscrapers of New York, stunned the corps of girls and rioting mobs below, awed the municipal troops on San Francisco's Upper Level, reverberated among the hills of its underworld.

They deafened the warring populace in New Orleans, Minneapolis, Denver, Boston, Detroit—every city and town of more than ten thousand population.

From each center of enunciation, across the surrounding countryside, in an ever-distending circle of sound that awoke the sleepers in little villages unscorched by the heat of revolution, swept the stupendous tidings:

"The Master is dead. His will makes the people his heirs to billions of gold."

CHAPTER TWENTY-FIVE

BESIDE the lounge on which lay the dead body of the Master, Dr. Edgerton, sitting with bowed head, stared at the sheet of paper spread on his knee. The first of its final directions he had fulfilled by throwing the heavy electric switch marked "No. 1" of the five the Master had pointed out in the drawer of the desk.

That had flashed the signal across the country for screaming sirens everywhere to compel attentive expectancy of astounding news. An immediate hookup of the nationwide radio network then broadcast. With maximum amplitude, the startling announcement that followed. It had long been ready for this crisis—a phonographic record filed in the station on top of the System building.

The Chosen Clique knew instantly what that stentorian proclamation implied. Now twenty thousand trustees of the

Master in cities, towns, villages, as they opened the duplicates of his testament, copied the formula for manufacturing gold, were learning the stupendous secret.

Already in newspaper composing rooms from coast to coast clicking, whirring typesetting machines were beginning to stamp that formula into the little metal lines that would print it in morning publications for millions to read.

Everyone could be rich. No skill was necessary, no hours of drudgery, no studious concentration. Application for eight or nine hours of a steady stream of cosmic rays from an ordinary ray-transformer to a mixture of lead with a few cheap chemicals produced virgin gold. The process was almost automatic. A child could superintend it.

In the sanctum of the Master the machines of communication worked unceasingly. From all parts of the country messages poured in; queries from every department of the System. To every one of these went back the same, short reply, an exhortation the Master himself had prepared:

"Try to maintain order." That was all.

Dr. Edgerton rose heavily, and walked to the eastern wall. The intern silently joined him, and together they looked out over the lake at the first splatter of dawn.

A sharp knock drew their attention away from the sunrise. They saw the commanding officer of the guard at the door. The doctor opened it.

The man's eyes were hot and greedy.

"We should have been relieved half an hour ago," he said, with unaccustomed arrogance in his voice, "but only three of the twelve who ought to be here have reported."

Dr. Edgerton glanced at the guards in the outer room. Their careless attitudes proclaimed relaxation of discipline.

He pretended not to notice this, and replied as casually as he could, "Three will be enough for the day. Tell them to lock the penthouse door after you and the others leave. We must have quiet here while arranging for the funeral."

Permission to go off duty surprised the officer, and for a moment he seemed indisposed to avail himself of it. Then he straightened his shoulders, and saluted.

Dr. Edgerton closed the door, and watched him speak to his command. The men listened sullenly, and left the penthouse slowly as if uncertain whether to obey.

As the morning advanced, lines formed at the Bureau of Private References in the System building. Hundreds presented cards calling for the instructions in cipher to be delivered on the death of the Master.

Few of the applicants were persons of importance. The Master had selected them from among the multitude of employees on the Upper Level because of characteristics other than financial acumen, business effrontery, or ability to make money. Most of them, men and women, received the same directions; to leave the metropolis.

A few short sentences advised some to start without delay by the private underground tube to the airport outside New City. Credentials were enclosed providing transportation and admission to the municipality.

The warning for others advised getting out into the open country at once. It disclosed the location of sites for new cities, and urged founding new communities. Help and instruction were promised.

Not one who received these directions gave them the slightest heed. Why leave the Upper Level when within reach for the first time was the means to satisfy every desire, to roll in wealth and luxury? Each tossed aside the Master's directions as inconsequential, and rushed to buy lead and other materials necessary for making gold.

Long before noon millions on the Upper Level and on the Lower Level were hard at work in quickly constructed laboratories in their homes. Everyone had a copy of the formula that seemed to promise unbounded riches.

Skeptics ridiculed this prospect. To make gold, they said, was impossible. They ignored what science had known for more than a century, that radium slowly changed into lead under the forces of nature; or, admitting this to be true, they denied that it was proof of a step toward transmutation into gold.

They laughed at the millions anxiously awaiting the outcome of experiments, and declared themselves to have been too constantly tricked by the Master during his life to be made fools of by him after his death.

But these scoffers met with a stunning shock in the early afternoon when a man, crazy with excitement, dashed into the Central Bank carrying a piece of heavy, yellow metal, and demanded to know if it were gold.

A careful assay demonstrated it to be gold of the finest quality.

Its owner hastily exchanged it for paper money, and rushed to the shops to buy.

And now thousands of experiments, started at dawn, began to culminate successfully. Within an hour the Upper Level was thronged with men and women carrying chunks of gold. Good-natured, laughing, eager crowds stormed the banks.

Supplies of the chemicals required in the manufacture of this new product dwindled away. Druggists and others who handled the materials tried to place orders for enormous quantities, but met with disturbing difficulties. Sálesmen, workers on lines of communication and in factories were quitting their jobs, indifferent to proffers of higher wages. The whole country was turning to the manufacture of gold.

Only in the banks did most of the employees remain earnestly industrious in their regular duties. Years of handling other peoples' money, and secondhand experience in financial affairs, had so infected them with confidence in the power of gold that merely to take it in at busy cashiers' windows in exchange for paper currency thrilled them with enjoyment and the sense of transacting important business.

At the usual hour the banks closed their doors against crowds struggling to get in. The tellers were exhausted. On the floor inside their cages lay pieces of gold in piles. The labor of removing it to the vaults was so arduous that minor clerks, janitors, window washers, scrub women, who still remained employees, were drafted in to help.

When evening came the Upper Level resounded with merrymaking. No guards stood at the entrances from the Lower Level to oppose admittance to the steady streams from the underworld. Everyone brought pieces of new-made gold.

Shops remained open. The proprietors seized the opportunity offered by eager buyers, to accept gold at a heavy discount in lieu of paper currency.

Theaters, cafes, and other places of entertainment were packed. Confusion caused by overcrowding was made worse by shortage of employees. Hundreds of attendants, waiters, chefs, servants in the kitchens, threw up their situations without so much as giving notice.

As the night advanced noisy revelry echoed among the high buildings of the downtown district. Intoxicated men and women danced in the streets. Residents of the Upper Level and the Lower Level mingled with enthusiastic protestations of equality, friendship and admiration.

But these revelers were only an insignificant fraction of the population. The millions were in their homes, patiently watching through the hours of the night the progress of innumerable experiments in the manufacture of gold.

The material most sought was lead. The stocks on hand had been snapped up at rising prices; but the demand was unappeased.

No matter how many experiments a person already had under way he hunted high and low the materials for more. On the Lower Level dwellers in houses and apartments tore out the plumbing to get lead pipe with which to enlarge their operations.

The women were as eager as the men in tearing up floors and digging into walls. In the early morning hours mobs on the Lower Level and bands of bravos on the Upper Level began to tear the lead pipe out of municipal buildings.

The reckless carelessness with which this destruction went on broke down the water system. Upper floors were drenched; cellars flooded.

At the first touch of dawn Dr. Edgerton opened the door in the floor of the sanctum. The intern and the two secretaries carried the body of the Master down into the room beneath. In one corner the doctor, following the posthumous directions, twisted a handle on the wall. A section in the floor slid to one side, exposing a leaden coffin.

They laid the Master's body in it, and fastened down the lid. The doctor reversed the handle on the wall, and the open section in the floor slid back into place.

The little funeral party returned to the sanctum, and Dr. Edgerton threw the second switch in the drawer of the desk. This released enormous voltage into an electric furnace many stories below the coffin. When the heat attained its maximum, the coffin dropped into the furnace and was instantly consumed.

All employees who had been engaged in the two corner penthouses had deserted their posts. Outside the sanctum a single guard moved about restlessly. Dr. Edgerton wrote an order releasing him from duty, and gave it to one of the secretaries to deliver.

The quartet left alone on the roof ate a silent breakfast of prepared food from a supply stored in the room beneath the sanctum, and Dr. Edgerton addressed the intern.

"You're free to go," he said, quietly.

The physician rubbed his head, thoughtfully.

"I can do nothing more here," he replied.

Dr. Edgerton accompanied him to the exit from the roof, locked the heavy door after his departure, and returned to the sanctum.

At the usual time the banks opened. For hours crowds had been waiting to get in. Men and women with as much gold as they could carry, struggled to hold positions in the long lines. There was less good humor than on the previous day; more rough elbowing and angry expostulation.

Everyone was keen to get quickly to a tellers window to exchange gold for paper money. Every minute's delay meant depreciation in its value. Prices were rising continuously. Shop keepers no longer would accept gold for currency. They were not assayers or bankers, they said. They sold goods for money, and wanted money in payment.

In the boulevards strangers mingled with the residents of the Upper Level and the Lower Level. The population of the countryside was swarming into the cities. Farmers left their fields; villagers, their little shops. They brought their families with them, overwhelming transportation facilities in the underground tubes and jamming the roads with their motor vehicles. All of them brought new-made gold.

They rushed to get currency for it to spend on luxuries that hitherto had been within the reach of millionaires alone. All the lead and other materials for the manufacture of gold in their own neighborhoods they had exhausted. Now they ransacked the cities for fresh supplies.

Prices leaped upward with accelerating speed. A loaf of bread cost one hundred dollars. The demand for paper currency became so great that the supply was inadequate. Merchants and shop keepers no longer would deposit their paper money in the banks, but hoarded it in secret places.

Factories closed down for want of workers. Employees in the great industries left their jobs and roamed the boulevards of the Upper Level, their pockets bulging with pieces of gold, in search of some place to exchange it for food.

Tens of thousands of dead bodies, lying at entrances to the Upper Level throughout the country, poisoned the atmosphere. No one would undertake the dreadful work of burial.

The Chosen Clique seized the Master's offices in the System building. Dispatches rushed back and forth from there to cities east and west, north and south. Recorded simultaneously on the machines in the sanctum on Ransler Castle, these communiqués informed Dr. Edgerton that conditions everywhere were desperate.

Ebets declared himself the successor of the Master. He grasped an empty sovereignty. No one opposed his supremacy, but his commands got little attention beyond the few retainers close around him. His assumption of leadership, however, made him the target for complaints and demands from every part of the country.

Food was the crying need. City after city sent demands, requests, and appeals for food. The shortage grew acute. Unless relief was forthcoming within a day or two, millions would face starvation.

The only response to these petitions of distress was vague promises, solicitous encouragement in empty words; but the requests had an evil effect. They emphasized the danger that lay ahead. Millionaires exerted all the power and influence they could still muster to gather food everywhere and store it in their palatial homes.

The numbers flocking in from the country increased the distress. Food no longer was for sale at any price.

The banks closed their doors. Their vaults were overflowing with gold. No one wanted it.

On the fourth day after the Master's death, messages to Ebets from New York and San Francisco, recorded on the machines in the sanctum, reported outbreaks of rioting.

Dr. Edgerton read these dispatches sadly, and went to the drawer in the Master's desk. Reluctantly he threw the third switch, dropped into a chair, and covered his face with his hands.

He had made use of the emergency switch to be used in case of war. It flashed a spark to myriad charges of super-explosives that mined the underground tubes around every city. Thousands in crowded trains approaching big centers of population were blown to atoms. The vast underground system of transportation was wrecked forever in a single moment.

Terrible confusion followed; but in the cities the masses applauded this destruction as a preventive measure against further crowding in from rural districts of millions whose continual arrival increased the danger of starvation for those already there.

No longer was there any semblance of order. Mobs began to plunder shops and warehouses with needless violence. They met no opposition, but fought among themselves. The commonest weapon in hand-to-hand melees was a slung shot hastily made by knotting a chunk of gold into a handkerchief.

What seemed to the mobs the most promising buildings to pillage, yielded the least spoil. Already the millionaires had removed the stores to their homes. The refrigerating plants of the meat packers were empty. The cold storage depots contained nothing to show for the record of supplies on their books.

The fury of innumerable mobs flamed into frenzy. They shouted that the multimillionaires were trying to starve the people. Attacks on villas and palaces along the Gold Coast began with a ferocity that grew more bestial every hour.

Crowds packed the boulevards on the near North Side from curb to curb, and roared for food and vengeance. Drunkenness aggravated the pandemonium.

On the fifth night after the Master's death rioters set fire to everything flammable, and made the night air—horrible with the stench of unburied corpses—ring with shrieks and laughter.

Bands of bravos that once powerful multimillionaires had been able to hold around them for protection by bribes of food, began to turn against their employers. They dragged them forth and threw them to the mobs. Unspeakable crimes were perpetrated until, as if nature itself revolted at the deeds of man, a deadly pestilence broke out in city after city.

It struck its victims first with infectious insanity that expressed itself in rollicking laughter, coarse jocularity, and gestures of wild merriment. This quickly gave way to a heavy stupor. Livid patches appeared on the faces and bodies of those stricken and they died grinding their teeth in agony.

The protective corps of Ransler Castle withstood the contagion of moral degeneration better than most such organizations; but it was not immune.

One at a time, and then in groups, its members deserted the household they had sworn to protect. They told the mobs of quantities of food in cellars and hidden storerooms of the castle, and themselves led the assault on the steel curtain that shielded the court of entrance.

In the sanctum Dr. Edgerton received frantic calls over the house phone. The mob was breaking in. The defenders were retreating up the stairways from the main door to the roof. The two deaf-and-dumb secretaries watched him with eyes that never questioned his authority. Simple souls, they knew only the habit of obedience. He sat waiting until the thunderous blows upon the door to the roof told him it could not much longer resist the onset of those trying to escape from the mob that pressed upon them.

Then he rose and stood beside the open drawer ready to throw the last two switches. One would release from thousands of pipes a flood of death-gas to deluge the miserable Upper Level and the underworld. The other would discharge mines of explosive beneath the System building. Ransler Castle and hundreds of other structures that towered throughout the country as monuments to the genius and power of the Master.

His eyes were steady, focused upon the door that gave entrance to the roof. He saw it tremble under a welter of blows and bound against its hinges. Then it crashed open, and Vivian Ransler, followed by a crowd of bravos and members of the household, came streaming across the roof toward the penthouse.

Dr. Edgerton waited no longer. With one quick glance at the two secretaries he threw over the fourth switch; and instantly afterward, the fifth.

A tremendous explosion split the atmosphere. Ransler Castle burst open from top to bottom like a rotten melon dropped on a pavement, and a huge belch of flame shot upward toward the sky.

CHAPTER TWENTY-SIX

On the calm esplanade just outside New City, Jimmy and Miriam watched the golden sun setting in the glorious colors of Indian Summer.

In front of them hardly a ripple scratched the glassy surface of the river. Behind them along the wide boulevard streamed motor cars filled with happy people. Lovers strolled together in blissful silence on winding paths under the trees and through the shrubbery.

In the distance, high in the air, heavy clouds of smoke hung above the broad circumference torn by super explosives into a deep gully that forbade approach.

Beyond this outer boundary, plague and famine hunted down mankind in the wrecked machinery of a civilization that was no more. Miserable survivors roved the open country in wretched bands. Their only aim was to flee from frightful spots of ruin and pest, once proud cities founded on confidence in the everlasting permanence of gold.

The smoke swayed and twisted in huge, grotesque shapes.

Miriam watched it with bright, sad eyes. It seemed like some giant diary of dreadful memories that gradually the wind would blow away—like shadowy representation of mighty forces in human nature, struggling in feeble instability.

Beside her on a bench near the edge of the stream, with her hand lightly clasped in his, Jimmy gazed at the red sunset and the pleasant shade of New City creeping toward them over the peaceful farms across the river.

He thought of Dr. Edgerton's lonely heroism, of the Master's ruthless humanity and courageous foresight. From before his own eyes the veil dissolved for an instant, and he beheld the future—a kindlier society in a better world.

The Senior Commissioner, approaching unobserved, felt the spell that held them.

"Our best artists," he said, with sympathetic understanding, "must be asked to prepare designs for a statue of the composite personality that shall do most to spread true civilization throughout the country, 'The Unknown Man of the Future.' "

Jimmy glanced at Miriam looking wistfully into the distance. "Why a man?" he asked, softly.

The Senior Commissioner nodded thoughtfully, and turned to the young girl.

"Miriam," he said, gently. "Miriam, your husband has made an excellent suggestion."

She roused herself from her dreaming, and looked at Jimmy with yearning tenderness.

"I did not hear," she murmured, without moving her eyes. "What is it?"

"I can best answer," replied the Senior Commissioner, with official dignity, "by delegating you to create the figure of an eager little child that shall be cast in heroic mould and shall stand in the heart of New City, symbolizing 'The Unknown Woman of the Future.' "

THE END

www.ingramcontent.com/pod-product-compliance
Lightning Source LLC
LaVergne TN
LVHW090940080826
845145LV00003B/835

* 9 7 8 1 6 1 2 8 7 2 3 1 5 *